TOO MUCH OF A GOOD
THING CAN BE MURDER!

"Come and see me work," said the Duchess, and Hardy followed her into her studio. There he stood watching her models as the Duchess arranged the strobe lights.

There was Gerrie, black and beautiful. Solveig, a natural for a blue-movie role as Miss Scandinavia. And Mee-ling, who gave the obvious lie to what they said about Chinese girls.

Vaguely Hardy wondered what they would look like with clothes on, but all thoughts faded as the Duchess posed them for her very candid camera. Here was a feast of good dirty fun to challenge even Hardy's extraordinary appetite . . .

. . . until he learned that he would also have to be a glutton for punishment, perversity and peril. . . .

Books by Martin Meyers

Patrick Hardy Mysteries

Kiss and Kill
Spy and Die
Red is for Murder
Hung up to Die
Reunion for Death

Dutchman Historical Mysteries
by Annette Meyers and Martin Meyers,
Writing as Maan Meyers

The Kingsbridge Plot
The High Constable
The House on Mulberry Street
The Lucifer Contract
The Organ Grinder
The Dutchman
The Dutchman's Dilemma

Visit us at www.speakingvolumes.us

HARDY

SPY AND DIE

Martin Meyers

SPEAKING VOLUMES, LLC
NAPLES, FLORIDA
2016

HARDY
SPY AND DIE

ISBN 978-1-62815-359-0

Chapter One

Patrick Hardy unbuttoned his shirt sleeve while Merle Doyle placed his jacket on a hanger and hung it up.

Hardy entertained himself by watching the lovely movements her rear end made as she walked.

While he watched he talked, "What else do you have in store for me today besides being checked out by you and your sphygmonometer?"

"The word is sphygmomanometer, and shut up, as usual you're talking too much."

"All right, blood pressure gauge, then, but . . ."

Her look as she wrapped the apparatus around his arm finally quieted him. She watched the gauge and listened, then switched to his other arm and watched and listened again. "I don't like it, Pat, your diastolic reading is over a hundred."

"Don't you understand? It's you. Can I help it if I have a big lech for my doctor who is stacked and beautiful and always ignores me."

"I'm not kidding, Pat, hypertension is nothing to laugh at. If we don't deal with it now it could cause you trouble."

"That's what it says on my card: Patrick Hardy, TROUBLE LIMITED."

She laughed and shook her head. "Oh, shut up. Grab your jacket and come into my office. . . . Where's your bracelet?"

"What bracelet?" he said and tried to open the top button of her white coat.

She lightly slapped his hand away and grinned. Dr. Merle Doyle was used to Patrick Hardy's nonsense, and really didn't mind it, as long as it didn't get out of hand. "Medical bracelet. Without that no one would ever know you were allergic to penicillin and a certified maniac."

"I think it's someplace in my desk at home."

"A good place for it. Come on. I want to give you a prescription. Your blood pressure is still too high, and you're letting your weight get up there too."

He pretended not to hear what she said about his weight and watched her body again as she led the way to her office. God, how he would love to make it with her.

Inside, the always going radio was playing a Beethoven sonata. Dr. Doyle ignored Hardy and listened.

"All right," he said, mimicking a soap opera character who has intimations of a terminal disease. "What is it? I can take it."

"No, you can't," she said. "Hypertension is not cancer or TB, but you've got to control it or it will start controlling you."

She wrote out a prescription, paused, thought for a few seconds and tore it up and wrote a new one. "I was going to give you a diuretic, but let's see if tranquilizers can do the job. They're fairly mild. Maybe they'll help you to cut down on your smoking . . . even quit completely. Take them three times a day. And try to cut out salt. Have Marie give you an appointment in two weeks."

She had forgotten him by now and was back to Beethoven.

He stopped by the drugstore to leave his prescription, bought a newspaper and walked to Riverside Drive. After an abnormally cool June, July had turned very hot. Hardy was all sweaty by the time he got home. His apartment, which was really two combined into one, was on street level and isolated from the rest of the building and, much to his joy, the rest of the tenants. He entered his private entrance, then after going through the procedure of disarming the alarms and undoing the many locks, he hurried into the office section of his apartment and immediately and compulsively started looking for his medical bracelet.

Between annoyed little searches, he turned up the air conditioner, relieved himself, washed up, and

7

changed his shirt. Sherlock Holmes, his black standard poodle, glanced tolerantly at his master from his resting place, and closed his eyes and went back to sleep. When Hardy moved the disarray from the top of his desk to the floor he stopped in irritation at not finding the bracelet and went into the kitchen and made himself a ham sandwich. Holmes joined him and was rewarded with a biscuit. With half the sandwich crammed in his mouth, Hardy resumed his search, this time with Holmes trying to get a share of the sandwich. He was taking a German beer stein from the bookcase when the doorbell and phone rang at the same time. Holmes started barking. Hardy barely managed not to drop the stein, yelled at Holmes to shut up, picked up the phone and said "hold on" and checked the TV monitor to see who was at his front door. All the while finishing off the last of his sandwich.

It was a man he had never seen before. Hardy pressed the speaker button and said, "Yes?"

The man, confused as to where the voice was coming from, looked around. "What is it?" Hardy demanded.

"Oh. Hey. That's wild. Kaplan live here?"

Hardy made a face. "Around the corner . . . the main entrance."

"Uh. Thanks." Now amused, Hardy watched as the man looked around for all the hidden equipment. The man peered and wiped at his neck and peered again. Remembering the phone, Hardy picked it up.

The man outside gave it all up and started for the corner. Hardy chuckled and said, "Hello."

"Well, that's what I call adding injury to insult. First you leave me dangling on the phone forever after saying 'hold on,' which is one of the most infuriating things that can happen to a person, and then when you finally come back to me, you laugh before you say hello. It would serve you right if I hung up and called another detective."

Her voice, despite the anger, had, minus the English accent, the same sexy, soothing quality of Glynis Johns'. And since Hardy had always had a thing for Glynis Johns ever since he had first seen her in the movies, he now automatically had a thing for this unknown female on the phone.

"No, wait. If you do that you'll never find out what I was laughing at, and I'll never get a chance to see if you're as pretty as your voice."

"Oh shit," she said surprisingly. "How corny can you get? Look, keep your fantasies to yourself. I need a detective, not a sex maniac."

Hardy couldn't resist. "It so happens I'm both."

He thought he could detect a bit of a smile in her voice. "Well, that's a little better than your first line. When can I come to see you?"

"What's wrong with right now?"

"Hey, that's great," she said sarcastically. "I'm glad that you can fit me into your busy schedule. I'll be there in fifteen minutes."

He hung up the phone and tried to remember what he had been doing before all the commotion

9

had started. Instead he thought about the voice on the phone and wondered about what went with it. Slight accent. Southwest. About twenty-five. Large firm breasts. Hardy had a thing about large firm breasts. He moved from his desk and lounged on the barber chair in front of the TV and turned it on. He recognized the movie immediately. *Aaron Slick from Punkin Crick*. Quickly, he switched channels. The only other movie on was a thing called *Zarak*. Hardy didn't mind looking at Anita Ekberg, but when she wasn't on the screen he lost interest and turned the TV off. He crossed to the bookcase imagining that his caller looked like Anita Ekberg. He reached for *The Best of Wilkie Collins* and nearly knocked over the beer stein. And remember what he had been doing.

He poured the contents of the stein on the table. A bugler's mouthpiece, a used 30 AMP fuse, a button from the Cloisters marked "M," a small incense candle. And . . . the medical bracelet.

Now if she would only look like Anita Ekberg, his day would be complete. He glanced at the barber chair and opted for the oversized black and brown velvet chaise next to his desk. Holmes joined him there. Hardy read the information on back of the bracelet: "Patrick Hardy. Allergic to Penicillin. Blood Type B. R.H.POS." With that he attempted to place the bracelet on his left hand. Several minutes later and thirty minutes after his phone call he was still trying to put the bracelet on when the doorbell rang. Of course Holmes barked. Thankful for the interruption, Hardy looked at the monitor.

10

Young, light hair, and very pretty. He wasn't sure about her figure yet.

He removed the bar of the Fox lock and went out into the hall. As he walked toward the front door, she examined him as defiantly as he examined her. When he opened the door Holmes pushed him aside.

"Hello, pooch. I'm Alice Henry. What's your name?"

"He's Sherlock Holmes and I'm Pat Hardy."

"Well at least one of you is a detective."

Hardy, who had turned to lead her into the office, turned back. The figure was good. Not Anita Ekberg, but enough to hold onto. "Oh shit," he said, "how corny can you get."

She tried to surpress the smile but it broke through. "We're going to get along just fine." Then she looked down and saw the doormat which said "GO AWAY" and said again, "Just fine."

Inside he got her a beer and himself a scotch and soda.

"Before we get down to business, Alice Henry, could you do me a favor and hook this thing together for me."

She glanced at the bracelet and quickly attached it to his left wrist. Then she examined the room, and taking her beer with her, sat on the barber chair. She looked at the room again, and its furniture and the pictures and said, "Very nice."

"Thank you, Ma'am" and he toasted her with his glass. "This your first time east?"

"No, believe it or not, I'm a Vassar girl. Two years

11

worth, anyway. It was all I could take. Don't say it.
... That makes me a half-Vassar girl."

"I wasn't going to. Where is home?"

She drank some beer and filled the glass again.
"This is good beer. I love beer on a hot day. You
tell me, you're supposed to be the detective."

"I'd say Oklahoma." When she didn't react he
hedged. "Near the Texas border."

"Hey, I'm impressed. Actually, it's the other way
around, I mean where I grew up was. Texas, near
the Okie border. A little town called Travis Corners.
I live in Houston now."

"OK," said Hardy, very pleased with himself.
"What's a nice young girl from Texas doing in a nasty
town like New York?"

"It's quite a story."

"Tell it."

She pointed to her empty glass.

While he got her second beer he freshened his own
drink.

"OK. The story." And he sat on the chaise.

"It all began when somebody killed my Uncle Walter."

"Alice Henry, you are a lovely young thing and I'd
love to take you to dinner and perhaps get to know
you better, but I do not handle murder cases. That is
strictly out of my league. Let the cops handle it."

"No need to get all worked up. The cops already
have handled it. That's why I'm here. It is a very
crazy story. And as long as I'm here drinking your
beer, why don't you let me tell it? Then if you don't

12

want the case, I'll find another detective and I'll take you up on dinner. And, if you do take the case, you still have to buy me dinner."

"Sounds like I'm being hustled, but go ahead."

"The whole silliness started when I got this letter from this law firm in N.Y." She set down her beer and pulled the letter out of her shoulder bag. "Allenberg, Edgarton and Black." Alice Henry placed the lawyer's letter on the stack table next to her and leaned back into the comfort of the chair. "This letter said that my uncle, Walter Henry, had left me some money and some other things, and his share of a jelly company over in New Jersey, Henry's Dietetic Jelly. You ever hear of it?"

Hardy pushed Holmes' nose out of his drink and scratched the animal's ear. "Nope."

"Neither have I. Here's where it starts getting silly. I never had an Uncle Walter. My father mentioned a brother, but I thought he was dead. Both my folks died when I was a kid and I was brought up by my Aunt Jessie. She died last year. As far as I knew I didn't have any other relatives. According to these lawyers, Uncle Walter was my only relative. I have a copy they gave me of a letter they have from my father to Uncle Walter telling him about me being born and where they were living and that they should forget the fight they had, whatever that was, and let bygones be bygones. I guess he didn't then, but he did in his will, 'cause he named me as his sole beneficiary, and since he has no other living relatives, the lawyers said except for the Internal Revenue people

13

getting their hands on what they think is their share, there should be no problem."

She sat up and finished off the beer in her glass, re-filled it partially with what was left in the bottle, and took another envelope from her purse, laying it next to the first one. "That's the copy of my father's letter I told you about. Where's the john?"

Hardy pointed. "Light switch is on the left. You always drink this much beer?" He hated beer.

"When I drink beer I do." And she closed the door.

Hardy read the two documents she had left on the table.

She was back. "What do you think?"

"I don't know. Seems all right to me. How do you keep looking like you do if you drink that much beer?"

"Oh," she smiled, sitting again, "I'm a very active person. This sure is a comfortable chair. Anyway, I said all right, luck is luck. I asked my boss for a few days off and came to New York. I've got to go back in a couple of days. But with this problem, I'll get to what it is in a minute, I need to be here or have some-body represent me here 'cause Mr. Hodges, that's my boss, he'd like to give me all the time I want, but he needs me in the store. I'm the buyer for women's sportswear, and it's very busy this time of year. But there's got to be somebody here, and that's where you come in—or will, I hope."

She stretched her arms, enjoying the chair. Hardy's glands and mind came to the same conclusion. She had a great-looking body. He squirmed in his chair,

14

trying to hide the fact that he had an erection, and at the same time, split-second fantasizing that she would notice and do something spectacular, like rip off his clothes in a sexual frenzy. He got up and walked behind her, adjusting his pants when he had the chance.

Well," she said, "will you help me?"

"Maybe," he said, walking clear into the living room and pretending to look out the window. He came back to the office and the chaise. "If you tell me how."

"That's the only trouble with beer, it makes me ramble so. The problem is, not that I'm an heiress, that's all right. The problem is when I asked the lawyers how he died, they said he was killed. . . . I said, 'Well, who did it?' They said it was being taken care of. I said, 'What do you mean it's being taken care of? Who do I call at the police?' They said it was not a police problem because my Uncle Walter was killed on a military installation, so it's a Federal matter.

"Well, I know it's the FBI who handles all those cases, I mean I've seen that on TV. So I asked, 'Who do I call at the FBI?' The lawyers finally gave me a number to call, but I couldn't get anyone there to tell me what was going on. Finally this fellow comes to see me at my hotel. He wasn't from the FBI, his credentials said something else, but he was government. He had me call the police commissioner's office to vouch for him, just so I would be sure in my own mind about him."

"Do you remember what department he was with?"

"No, it wasn't CIA, but he was a government man. The police backed him up on that. I remember there

15

was an eagle on his card, in the center, very faint," she went into her bag again, "same as this one on a dollar bill. Well, up until this time I was wondering if maybe all these fellows were phonies and this was some sort of confidence game. Real, they are real . . . but it is a very unreal situation. Anyway, he said my uncle was found dead on this post, didn't tell me how he was killed. After they did an autopsy he was cremated according to his own last wishes. But this agent, or whatever he was, said he couldn't tell me any more because of security reasons."

"There's your answer," Hardy told her. Security. Take your money and run back home to Houston. Security is the magic word in this country. From what you've told me, it seems like that's the end of it. Security."

"No, it's not," she said. "It all seems kind of funny to me. This fellow says they're doing what they have to do but that's all they're going to tell me. Well, that sounds like a lot of double talk. I want some answers. I never knew I had an Uncle Walter. But now that I do know it, I know that somebody's got to find out who killed him. If the authorities won't, I will. At least, maybe you will, for me. . . . Does that make any sense? Don't answer that. Can I have another beer?"

He gave her the beer, and as he did, his mind tugged at a memory of something she had said. While he ran it through his mind he made a mental note about taping his office conversations.

When Hardy looked up again, Alice Henry's drink

16

was gone and Holmes was slurping up the remains of his. "Get away, you lush. Sorry, I was concentrating."

"I noticed."

"That agent talks too much."

"What do you mean?"

"The lawyers told you the body was found on a military installation. That could have meant a lot of things. Shipyard, supply depot, a lot of places. But your friend with the eagle card didn't say military installation, he said post, that narrows things down for us."

"I think you'll do. What time do you want me to be ready?"

"Huh?"

"For dinner?"

"Seven-thirty. You like French food?"

"I love it. I'm at the Gotham House."

When she was gone he turned the TV on, then turned it off in disgust at the lack of good movies. He was hungry. In deference to his doctor's reminder about his weight, Hardy chose yogurt over banana cream pie and milk. As he lit a Marlboro, he remembered her nagging about cigarettes too.

"To hell with it," he said to Holmes as he fed the dog. "Live dangerously, that's what I always say."

Chapter Two

Tony led them to their table. "Something to drink, Mr. Hardy?"

Hardy said to Alice Henry, "This place makes the best daiquiris in the world."

"OK, but just one."

"Two daiquiris," he said and Tony was off.

They talked about plays and movies until the drinks came.

"That *is* good," she said.

"They add a dash of Cointreau. Say, I know I offered you French food, but this place makes a great steak."

"No, thank you. I was promised French food. I get French food."

Tony was back and Hardy gave him their order.

Later, as they had their cheese and coffee, Alice sighed, "You were right. Very nice. Can I have a cigarette?"

"I didn't realize you smoked."

"Not often," she said.

He immediately rejected the notion of the Paul Henried-Bette Davis cigarette lighting scene and lit theirs in a normal manner.

They walked out of the cool restaurant into the hot street. Alice took Hardy's hand and said, "Now you can walk me home and tell me that you're taking the case."

"Yes to one, no to two."

"Then I'll have to convince you."

"But why not?" she said for the umpteenth time as they rode up in the elevator.

"Because I'm chicken. Especially when there's been a murder. Besides, you can't afford me. Two hundred a day."

"Yes, I can. I'm an heiress."

She opened her own door. "Turn on the air conditioner, please. I thought all private detectives ate nails for breakfast." She double-locked the door.

He couldn't help but laugh at her actions. "What are you going to do, offer me your body in exchange for taking the case?"

She laughed back. "Don't be so sure of yourself. You're cute, but it takes more than cute for me to make it with someone." She was in the bathroom and since she hadn't closed the door, Hardy could see her removing a plastic bag that was secreted in her bath

19

powder. "I hope you turn on, Pat, because if you don't it'll be a real drag."

Hardy was a square pothead. He had smoked grass before, but for him it was only an occasional pastime. He only turned on when someone else had it, and then only indoors and with people he liked.

Playing Mr. Cool, he answered, "I turn on" and watched intently and admiringly as she hand-rolled two joints of marijuana with great expertise.

"Here," she said. "You do the honors. It's great stuff, and all from the top of the plant." He took several deep drags. "Don't be greedy, besides I don't want you to get too far ahead of me," she said and took the cigarette from him.

"How could I get ahead of a head?"

"Give me a few minutes and I'll tell you." She kissed him and exhaled smoke into his mouth.

He felt good. He liked her and she seemed to like him and there was no one hiding in any of the closets. That thought bothered Hardy. Just to be sure he made the rounds of all the closets and looked.

Music was playing and Alice Henry was dancing to it. Hardy joined her and they finished off the rest of the cigarette. Time seemed to progress like a movie with some of the frames cut out.

She had a beautiful body. When had she taken off her clothes? When had he? They made it on the floor.

"Pat, you're scratching me with that damned bracelet."

Pat was busy.

A serene detachment took over and time seemed

20

to slow down. And in between motion he looked down at the young body moving feverishly under his. Not Anita Ekberg but they were lovely breasts. He leaned over and put his mouth to one and then the other as the movements continued super-quick in the slow-motion world he was living. "I love to ball on hot nights," she moaned.

His hands moved to the gyrating hips that were helping him run his race. He pulled her closer to him. Explosion. What was that song she was singing? Again, another peak, and release and relief. He lay there resting and admired the two women next to him. Two women? Alice smiled at him and snuggled closer. "Do you like French cooking?" and put her hands between his legs.

"Hmmm," said Hardy as her manipulations proved effective. But the other woman. She just lay there. Peg just laid there. But Peg was from another time and another place and didn't belong there at all. A long time ago there had been Peg, and a man with a gun and a frightened fat man, and a frightened thin man with a scar on his stomach.

But Peg was gone and Hardy pushed her out of his mind and out of the bed. He opened his eyes and looked. She was gone.

When Hardy awoke again, it was in his own bed. He lay there in that semi-state between asleep and awake and recalled the night-long marathon. Peg. The funny thoughts and memories that a little pot will bring to the surface. He fingered the scar on his stomach and tried to forget that memory immediate-

21

ly. He concentrated on remembering how much he could of the real things that had happened. "Wow. That kid was too much." A part of his mind was annoyed when it considered that she had put the make on him and not the other way around.

He also remembered that she had thrown him out in the early morning and said she was flying back to Houston and would phone him in a couple of days to get his decision about taking the case.

"Goddamn all women." He didn't want the stupid case. And despite the inducements, he wasn't going to take it. And that was final.

He was hungry. Thoughts of not working out and having an immediate giant breakfast came to him. He looked in the full-length mirror. There was a hint of a spare tire on his otherwise pretty good physique. Vanity rather than good sense won out and he went into the little gym next to his bedroom. A workout, a shower and ten buckwheat cakes and six rashers of bacon later, Holmes barked Laura in. "Morning, Mr. Hardy." She gave him his mail, tuned in the appropriate soap opera and started her cleaning chores. Hardy took his coffee and mail to his office. The mail was mostly junk except for one letter from a department store client. They had hired Hardy after their own security people had failed. In two weeks he discovered that one of the store's own managers had brought in his own cash register. No one ever noticed that there were five instead of the official four.

There was a note from the president of the firm expressing gratitude and a check with a lot of zeros on it. Hardy filed the letter and after writing "for deposit only" on the check put it in his pocket with his checkbook.

"Laura," he yelled from the door.

She turned off the vacuum cleaner. "Yes?"

"Let the service answer the phone. I'll be back in about a half hour." Holmes danced around the hall, impatient to go out.

"Yes, Mr. Hardy." And he heard her warn one soap opera person about another and start vacuuming again.

Another hot day. The street was empty. Except for the red-haired man coming toward him. The one with a knife.

Holmes growled.

"Shut that dog up or I'll stick both of you."

"Sure, anything you say," and Hardy felt the pancakes and bacon and his own acids coming up. He reached to give Red Hair his watch.

Red Hair took this for a hostile action and slashed at him.

Pancakes and bacon and acids and fear were gone.

Hardy grabbed at the offending knife-wielding arm and broke it. Red Hair dropped the knife, looked in amazement and screamed in pain. He grabbed up the knife with his good hand and turned and ran. Hardy chased after him, tripped in a pothole and fell. The fall jarred him back to his senses and Red Hair got away. Hardy checked the status of his trick left knee and shook as waves of fear took over his body. The Army had taught him how to fight reflexively but had never been able to teach him how not to be afraid.

Holmes stood over him and licked his master's face. "Hello, coward, take this coward's hand." Holmes licked some more.

Hardy skipped the bank and went straight to the drugstore for his tranquilizers. At home he gave Laura the rest of the day off. He popped two capsules, informed the police of what had happened, took a hot bath and massaged his aching knee, popped one more capsule, and with the complete works of T.S. Eliot went straight to bed.

Chapter Three

Morning. No dreams. Head clear. Knee fine. Just to make sure he spent most of his workout on leg exercises.

Ride the High Country was on Channel 5. He watched it while he ate breakfast. It was the fourth time he had seen it.

The doorbell rang during the shootout and Hardy's third cup of coffee. Annoyed, he scanned the entrance. Detective Second Grade Gerald Friday stood there impatiently. Hardy considered not answering as he watched the black cop ring the bell again.

"Goddamn it, Holmes, shut up." He turned off both TV screens and went to the door. They nodded hello to each other and Hardy led him back in. "This is an unexpected pleasure."

"Unexpected I know, pleasure I doubt. Christ, will you look at this place! If the real cops in this town could see this place . . ."

"Yes?"

"Never mind, Mr. Private Detective." He eyed Hardy with distaste. "Private Detective."

"Then you're here to arrest me for attacking that mugger."

"What mugger? The commissioner's office has asked me to pay you an unofficial visit. The purpose of the visit is to request that you do not take the Walter Henry case."

"Uh oh, Big Brother is watching me. Why?"

"Security reasons, and as a favor."

"It's become the fashion in this country to use that word for any reason, and since when are we on favor terms?" The whole turn of events bothered him. He was all set not to take the case, now this. His mouth made polite conversation while his brain tried to think. "You want something to drink? I haven't seen you for a while. Have they put you in charge of the precinct yet?"

Friday lit a cigarette. "I'll have a Coke. I'm not with the precinct anymore. I'm with Manhattan North. Are you going to lay off?"

Hardy went to the kitchen. "Who's asking?"

"I told you."

He brought in the Cokes and a bowl of cashews. "No, I mean who's asking them to ask you to ask me?"

"That's classified information," said Friday. He

took a handful of nuts and continued. "Crap. I haven't got time to play word games with you the way your paperback cops do. There seems to be some question about your license. Somebody made a mistake about your qualifications when it was issued. Five weeks of setting on your ass in an MP outfit doesn't exactly come under the heading of 'former police experience.' "

"Boy," said Hardy. "this must really be something for you to go and pull my 201 file. You know you can't revoke my license on something as flimsy as that. If you're going to threaten me, at least use something that's scary."

Friday kept chewing nuts and drinking Coke and getting more and more agitated. "How about the Federal Government?"

"Now that's scary."

"You'd make wise-ass remarks at your own funeral. ... What mugger?"

"Yesterday. Male. Caucasian. Red hair. Stocky. About thirty years old."

"I'm impressed with your powers of observation. Any distinguishing marks?"

"Yes, a dangling right arm. I broke it for him."

"Sure you did."

"I told the fellow at the precinct what happened. Check it out. Anything else, Detective Friday?"

"What's the matter, getting tired of my company?"

"I'm impressed with your powers of observation."

"Goodbye, Private Detective. By the way, in your Army file, before you were with the MPs, it says you were given special training, but it doesn't say what kind."

"So."

"Well, what kind?"

Hardy opened the door. "That's classified information."

"Very funny. Very funny."

Before he could get his mind organized, the phone rang.

"Hello."

"Hello, Pat. It's me, Alice."

"You've got yourself a private detective," and as soon as he said it he wanted the words back, but Alice didn't give him time to say anything else.

"Pat, that's marvelous. I'll send you a check. Can't dawdle, I'm in a rush. Pat . . . ?"

"Yes."

"I miss you. Goodbye."

He hung up the phone. "Now why the hell did I do that?"

Holmes stared at him and kept quiet. Hardy patted the dog on the head and took a tranquilizer. He knew the only reason he had taken the case was because Friday asked him not to. Now he was stuck. He reached for the cashew nuts, found the bowl was empty and went into the kitchen for more. He munched nuts and drank Coke and sat at his desk swinging in half-circles on his swivel chair. After twenty minutes or so of this, he sighed and dialed information for the number of Allenberg, Edgarton and Black.

He told the switchboard operator who he was and why he was calling. She switched him to Mr. Black's secretary and he told her who he was and why he was calling.

"I'm afraid Mr. Black is in conference now. Could he call you back?"

"What about Mr. Edgarton?"

"He's in the same conference."

"And Mr. Allenberg . . ."

"Is in the same conference," they said together.

"OK," said Hardy, trying a new tack. "What's your name?"

"Melissa Howard."

"What are you doing for lunch?"

"I'm going shopping. If you would give me your number, Mr. Hardy . . ."

"Maybe Mr. Allenberg or Mr. Edgarton or Mr. Black will return my call."

"Yes, sir."

He didn't disconnect when she hung up. As he hoped, the switchboard operator came on the line. He said, "This is Mr. Hardy. I was just talking to Melissa and . . ."

"I'll ring her back for you."

"No. Don't bother. Uh, say, what's your name?"

He heard another phone pick up.

"Her name is Rita Harte, Mr. Hardy. Mrs. Rita Harte and she has a switchboard to run. I'll see that Mr. Black gets your message. Goodbye, Mr. Hardy."

"Goodbye, Miss Howard."

Annoyed at himself for being impatient and for attempting a ploy that was unnecessary and stupid, and annoyed because the ploy failed, he dialed his own number. He listened to three busy signals and hung up.

The phone rang. "Hi, stud."

"Hi, Ruby." Hardy's face lit up as he spoke. Ruby was a striper with a fantastic body and she was a very good friend.

"Hey, stud, you still have it?"

"It's always with me. I can always get my hands on it."

"That's no fun. Wouldn't it be better if I had my hands on it?"

The remark brought on the expected reaction. "Where are you, Red?"

"I'm doing a convention in Philadelphia, then I have to go to Toronto. Why don't you drive down and make Philadelphia a nicer place to be?"

He thought about Alice and his new job for about five seconds. "What time and where, Ruby?"

He stopped by his garage to tell them to have his VW ready and sent up to 84th Street to his favorite Szechuan Chinese restaurant. When he went in he had the vague feeling that he was being followed. After a paranoid lunch of sauteed hot beef shreds and sliced prawns with garlic sauce he left and walked aimlessly uptown crossing the street erratically, back and forth. On his second back and third forth not only did he know he was being followed but he knew it was by two separate men. Number one was Mr. Average wearing gray lightweight summer pants and a blue sports jacket. Number two, short and dark, with a mustache and a chest like a bull, wore a brown suit. Hardy thought he looked Egyptian.

He reversed course and headed home, stopping long enough to buy natural sugar at a health food store and a paper and the new *Playboy*. When he turned the corner to Riverside Drive his tails were still there.

He finished reading "The Advisor," shook his head at the idiots who wrote to it and turned to look at the centerfold. His appreciation of the lady's figure and coincidental thoughts of Ruby's were bothered by the phone.

"Hello."

"Mr. Hardy. There is a pay phone one block from your house. Do you know the one I mean?"

"Yes."

"Will you please go to it?"

"Why?"

"Mr. Friday didn't think the word security was sufficient for you, but it's the only one I have."

"Five minutes," said Hardy.

"Thank you."

He scanned the area as he waited for the booth phone to ring. Brown Suit was sitting in the park reading a paper, but he couldn't spot Blue Jacket. The phone rang. "Hello."

"Who is this?"

"Oh, for God's sake. If I can recognize your voice, you can certainly recognize mine."

31

"Your inability to conform was noted in your Army file."

"When did my file get on the best-seller list?"

"Mr. Hardy, my name is George Archibald. On behalf of the United States, I now ask you not to have anything to do with the Walter Henry case."

"Sounds great. But who the hell are you? For all I know this could be a Commie plot."

"I am not at liberty to tell you any more, but I offer Mr. Friday and his superiors as my bona fides."

Silence.

"Mr. Hardy?"

"OK, I guess so. Another thing, you better teach your people how to tail better."

"It was meant to be an open surveillance."

"OK, if you say so, but isn't it gilding the lily to use two men?"

"What do you mean?"

As he described the two men, Hardy realized why Mr. Archibald was asking. "The guy in the brown suit, he's not one of yours, is he?"

"No. Can you still see him?"

"Yes, and I'm pretty sure he knows it."

"Stay in that booth and act as if you're still talking for at least fifteen minutes, and then go about your own business."

"Right, and in case you're interested, I'm going to Philadelphia to get laid. I hope that isn't a violation of security." But he was talking into a dead phone.

Five minutes later Brown Suit got up and glared at the phone booth and then looked around suspiciously and left. Hardy rejected the notion of following him and went back to his apartment. He gave Holmes an early dinner, grabbed a toothbrush, and allowed himself to think only about Ruby.

The route downtown to the Lincoln Tunnel was bumper to bumper. He cursed at the silver Mercedes that cut him off entering the tunnel and wished he owned it. He wondered if it were air-conditioned.

He saw it again just ahead of him in another lane but was distracted by a marvelous-looking young girl who buzzed by on a motorcycle.

When he saw the car again, he was leaving the Jersey Turnpike. He wasn't sure it wasn't a coincidence but he was sure enough to be worried. He aimed his car for the Pennsylvania Turnpike and kept as much space between the car ahead and himself as he could. As the car ahead came abreast of the ticket booth, Hardy pulled out of line and darted for the regular road. He hoped there were no state troopers around to react to his erratic behavior. Also, he was pleased to see that the Mercedes had no choice but to go onto the turnpike.

His pleasure was short-lived when he drove into Philadelphia and saw the silver car fall in behind him. He also saw that the driver was his friend in the brown suit.

First movie house he spotted, Hardy parked and went in. After checking which side door he was going to use, he bought some popcorn and watched what was on the screen. It was an unentertaining cartoon which showed cans of paint invading a house and

33

covering it in haphazard multicolors. He shelved his thoughts of Tom and Jerry and Bugs Bunny and watched the door. If Brown Suit didn't come in soon he would have to leave anyway.

Brown Suit came in. As quietly as possible, Hardy scooted out the side door. There was no one near his VW or the Mercedes which was parked nearby. Hardy hummed a phrase of a song and got into his car. He turned the key. The car made noises, but wouldn't start. He accepted the fact that Brown Suit wasn't as dumb as he had hoped and left his car and started walking. Hardy put on his sunglasses and took off his jacket. At the corner he looked back and saw Brown Suit on the street, looking around. He stepped into a doorway and watched. Brown Suit smiled and got into his car and drove away. Hardy was sure he wasn't going too far and that if he went near his car he would have company again. On the next street he found a gas station.

"Hi," he said to the man sitting inside the office.

"What can I do for you?"

"You the owner?"

"Yeah, I'm Pete Nevins. What can I do for you?"

Hardy showed him his driver's license and resisted showing his detective license. "My name is Pat Hardy. I've got a VW two streets back. . . . Across from the Clark movie house. Loose distributor wire or something like that. You got a toilet?"

The man gave him a key attached to a piece of wood and pointed. "Just around the corner."

Hardy checked the area before going in and after

34

coming out. Pete Nevins was busy with a customer. Hardy went into the office and bought himself a Coke and waited for him.

"There you are. What's the number on that Volkswagen?"

"Here, I've written it down, and here are my keys and here's fifty dollars. . . . If it's more, I'll settle with you tomorrow. Do you think you can have it for me?"

"If it's only what you say it is, I can have it for you as soon as my brother comes back and I can get over there to look at it." He fingered the bill and examined it. "This'll more than cover it."

"That's fine," said Hardy. "I don't think I can wait around. You have a card?"

Nevins gave him one. "Thanks," said Hardy, "I'll call you and let you know when I'm picking it up." On an impulse he stopped at a pay phone and called the police and pretended to be the owner of a stolen Mercedes. He gave Brown Suit's license number and hoped Philadelphia police were as efficient as they were supposed to be.

He told the cab driver to drop him anywhere on Market Street. From there he took a bus a few stops and then another cab to Ruby's hotel.

Ruby's last name was Rose. Hardy asked at the desk.

"Are you Mr. Hardy?"

He nodded.

The desk clerk smirked. "Miss Rose said that you would be coming by and that I was to give you the key. She said that you were her cousin."

Hardy took the key. "What's the matter, don't you see the family resemblance?"

The clerk thought this was very funny and had a giggling fit. Hardy took the elevator to the fifth floor. Inside he stripped and took a shower, drank some of Ruby's scotch and got in bed and read the bible he found in the nighttable drawer.

He was dreaming about Ruby. She was wearing a net bra and a G-string and her red hair was flowing wildly. She was calling him. "Come on, stud. Let's go."

"Come on, stud, time to wake up."

He opened his eyes. "Hi, Red." He grinned at her. "What do you want me to do, start without you? Put that luscious body in bed next to mine."

"Sorry, stud. I guess I lost track, but it's that time of the month. Don't get sore, I only realized it myself a half hour ago. Hey, you better put some clothes on if you're going to go away mad."

"For your information, I am going to take a shower, a cold shower."

She chuckled, "Do you want company?"

"No thanks."

During their dinner of shrimp fiorentina, he told her what had been happening.

"Sounds like a lot of trouble that you'd be better off without. Come with me to Toronto, Pat. In a few days I'll be able to make up for tonight. I'm only booked for a week, then I have some free time. We could just kid around for a while."

"Sounds tempting, but there's nobody around to take care of Holmes. Tell you what. When I get back to New York I'll call Alice Henry and tell her the government says to lay off. Then I'll get someone to adopt my dog for a while, and I'll meet you in Toronto."

"That's marvelous." She drank some wine and touched his hand. "I can hardly wait."

"Cut it out, will you, I'm frustrated enough as it is."

"I'm sorry, Pat."

"Forget it. It's not you. I have to figure out how to get my car and get back to New York. . . . The smartest thing would be to forget the car and fly back and tell that guy to store it for me."

Ruby lit a cigarette and gave it to him. "How do you know the man in the brown suit even knows where your car is? Don't you think your call to the police did any good?"

Hardy took a drag of the cigarette, then absent-mindedly snuffed it out. "Of course he knows where it is. He's smart. And the smart thing to do if he wants to find me is keep tabs on my car. Unless I don't use my car. Unless this is so big he has people at the airport and the railroad. What the hell is this? Sounds like a James Bond movie. Unless the police did stop him and he ran and they shot him, and he's dead. No such luck. He probably has a cover story a mile long and they apologized for bothering him, that is if they ever even stopped him. I wish I knew if he's just keeping track of me or if he's after me. He might be alone. Then he'd have to stick with the car. I'll take a plane."

They went back to her room.

"Pat, what are you doing?"

"Washing my shirt."

"When did you become such a Mr. Clean?"

"When people like Brown Suit and you in your god-damned shorty nightgown make me sweat for different reasons. Besides, it's good therapy. You have any tranquilizers? I would have brought my own, but I didn't think I'd need them."

She had put a robe over her scant nightgown. "Here, try one of mine." She handed him a couple of small yellow pills. "I use them sometimes when I have to get to sleep."

Hardy swallowed both and washed them down with water.

He took the bedspread to the couch.

"Don't be silly," she said, "we'll share the bed."

"No thank you, sweet breasts. Even with the wine and . . ." He yawned ". . . those yellow things I took, lying next to you and not touching you would be torture."

"You're a nice horny toad. Goodnight, Pat."

He yawned again. "Goodnight, Ruby."

Chapter Four

When he awoke from a restful dreamless sleep, it was ten o'clock. There was an eyebrow pencil note from Ruby on the bathroom mirror: "The room is yours till one. I ironed your shirt. Can't wait till Toronto. Don't ever ask me to marry you, I might say yes. Love, R."

He chuckled and wiped the writing away and made a face at himself in the mirror.

After a barbershop shave and breakfast, he called Pete Nevins.

"Hello, Mr. Hardy. To tell the truth, all I had to do was put in a new rotor."

"What was wrong with it?"

"Nothing, somebody removed it."

Hardy touched his throat where the barber had shaved too close. "Was anybody looking for me?"

"You mean that short guy . . . the one with the mustache? Was he the one who stole your rotor? Look, I don't want to get in the middle of anybody else's fight. I got my own troubles."

"Don't worry," said Hardy, "there'll be no trouble. What happened?"

"I told the short guy you went to California and wouldn't be back for two weeks. Looked like a real jerk to me. I didn't like him at all."

"Thanks, I appreciate it. Is he still hanging around?"

"No."

Hardy knew it would be smarter to stick to his original plan and take a plane back to New York.

"Mr. Nevins. . . . Does that fifty dollars entitle me to any more service?"

"Depends."

"Could you park my car on the corner of Sixth and Walnut, leave my keys on the floor and go into the Liberty Bell Room in Independence Hall and hang around for about five minutes as if you're waiting for someone? Will you do that for me?"

"Why not?"

"Thanks a lot. I know this seems kind of crazy but . . ."

"Forget it," said Pete Nevins. "You know something, I've lived in Philadelphia all my life, and I never been to Independence Hall. How do I find the Liberty Bell Room?"

"Ask anyone," said Hardy. "You can't miss it."

An hour later Hardy stood among a group of sight-seers. He watched his bug pull up and Pete Nevins get out. Nevins padded his part by tossing a set of keys in his hand as he crossed toward Independence Hall. Hardy hoped the man *was* padding his part and that they weren't really the keys to the VW.

Quickly Hardy moved to the car. Once in he searched the floor. "Damn it. Nevins, if you . . ." He stopped his mumbling when he saw the keys in the ignition. Hardy shrugged and drove to the Benjamin Franklin Bridge. Satisfied that the Mercedes was not following, he stopped in Camden for a hamburger and took the Jersey Turnpike to New York.

He parked the car midtown and took a bus home. On the bus he found a discarded copy of the *News*. There was a short uninformative story in it about the body of a man being found in the boat basin of Riverside Park. The description sounded like Archibald's man with the blue jacket.

Hardy was sweating and his eyes were itching. He greeted Holmes with a perfunctory pat on the head and gulped down several glasses of orange juice.

The phone rang. Three rings and it stopped. He took a tranquilizer with the last of the juice, determined to let the answering service take all of his calls. The phone rang again. This time it didn't stop after three rings . . .

"Shut up, Holmes, I hear it. . . . Hello."

"Mr. Hardy . . . Don't blame your answering service for not picking up, we told them not to. Do you recognize my voice today?"

"Yes."

"Good. I would like you to leave your apartment and . . ."

"Look let's forget it, huh. I quit. I am no longer concerned with what happened to Walter Henry."

"I'm sorry," said Mr. Archibald. "I'm afraid it's too late for that. You will leave your apartment and walk downtown on Broadway until you are contacted. The recognition signal is 'Nevermore.' Is all that clear?"

"Christ, cloak-and-dagger time. What if I refuse?"

"In a matter of hours you would be back in the Army and unable to refuse."

"I'll give your regards to Broadway." And he hung up.

Bolstered by another tranquilizer he started downtown. At Lincoln Center he stopped for a frankfurter and a drink. He was admiring rainbows formed by the spray of the fountain when the man came up to him. "Goddamn it. Do you think this is a picnic?"

Hardy backed off in panic. "Huh?"

"Never," said the man.

Hardy kept his distance and looked around.

"I said never."

"Oh," said Hardy. "More . . . more. Nevermore."

"Come on," and the man trotted down the steps to a car. Hardy followed and got in. They drove in silence to the Sheraton Hotel. The man parked the car and they walked through the hotel and out to 56th Street. A second car pulled up and they got in and drove in silence again.

The second car dropped them on 35th Street and

drove away. Hardy's new friend led him to a building halfway down the block. After depositing Hardy on a freight elevator and pressing five, he went back out to the street.

Hardy was met on the fifth floor. "Hello, Mr. Hardy, I am Mr. Archibald."

Hardy recognized the lean dapper man by his voice. Still, "Never."

"More," said Mr. Archibald, the hint of a smile tugging at his lips. "I know it all sounds like a movie melodrama but it's all very necessary, I assure you. This way, please."

The man at the desk was fat. Fatter than Hardy had been years before when a would-be killer's bullets had shown him how to lose weight fast. "Is this the idiot?"

"Yes, sir," said Mr. Archibald. "Mr. Hardy, this is my boss, Julius Foxx."

"Mr. Hardy," said Foxx, "would you mind telling us what the hell you think you are doing? Never mind, I'll tell you. You have barged in where you weren't wanted. You have disrupted a very important mission which concerns the welfare of your country and you might very well have been the cause of the death of one of my men."

"I read about that. I'm sorry. But look, now that I understand, I'll stop. I didn't mean to get in your way."

Foxx took a cigar from a case on the desk and rolled it in his hands. "You can't stop now. The situa-

43

tion now demands that you continue your investigation."

Hardy sat down. "But I don't want to."

Between puffs of smoke Foxx told him, "I'm afraid you have no choice in the matter." He opened a folder. "Patrick Hardy, 51258727. According to your record, the government spent a lot of money on your training. No matter your own feelings, you were trained to react reflexively and to fight and kill if necessary when attacked. Show me."

Hardy rubbed his itchy eyes. "If you read the whole thing you also know the whole experiment was a failure."

"Come now, Lieutenant."

"Crap. They made us all second lieutenants. It was supposed to give us incentive."

Mr. Foxx nodded to Mr. Archibald. Hardy felt Archibald's arm starting to tighten around his neck. Hardy slipped to the floor and out of the grip. Using the chair as a battering ram, he smashed Archibald into the wall. When Foxx tried to chop him in the neck, he elbowed him in his ample stomach and was about to break his nose and push the broken shards into the fat man's brain when the two men who had entered grabbed him.

Several minutes of thrashing about segued into several seconds of glassy-eyed calm. "I'm all right, you can let go," said Hardy, "except I think I'm . . ."

Archibald opened the door to a washroom.

When he came out, Hardy lit a cigarette. His hand was shaking. "Satisfied? I must be getting old. Not as

44

fast as I was. There was a time when the two of you would have been in much worse shape."

"Nevertheless," said Foxx, who was now back at his desk and breathing heavily as he lit a new cigar, "very impressive. Mr. Hardy, I can tell you almost nothing. I can tell you that if you don't cooperate you will jeopardize a mission that is very important to the welfare of your country. You have bungled right into the middle of that mission. I must admit that this was through no fault of your own. But now that you're in, you must stay in."

"That's it?" asked Hardy. "I really don't mind helping out, but that's like asking a blind man to drive a car."

"Not a brilliant analogy, but apt enough. Mr. Archibald will see that you get home."

"Wait a minute, Mr. Foxx. Let me get this straight. What exactly do you want me to do?"

"You will continue your investigation for Miss Henry into the death of her uncle, Walter Henry. Eventually when you are unable to find his murderer, you will report that to Miss Henry and then as far as you are concerned the case will be closed."

"And what if I do find out who murdered him?"

Mr. Foxx savored his cigar. "Then you'll be a better man than I give you credit for."

Hardy followed Archibald to the door and stopped. "Who's the short dark man with the mustache?"

Foxx looked at the gray ash of his cigar. "His name is Joseph Korboff. He is very dangerous. Good luck."

Archibald spoke to him in the hall. "To answer

your next question, Mr. Hardy, our organization has existed for some time. As a matter of fact, up until last year we didn't even have a name, we just were. The President needed a designation for us so he dubbed us the Central Security Force, C.S.F." Archibald smiled. "We do have a penchant for initials in this country. . . . However, I doubt if anyone will ever see that name on any official papers. It's just a means of designation. Except for the President, very few people even know of our existence. There are no records of us, not even pay records. Our expenses are skimmed off every other venture that this government has, all the way from rocketry maintenance to indigent poor food costs. . . . Please Mr. Hardy, no moral comments. No Watergate dialogue. What has to be done is done. We are responsible to no one except Mr. Foxx, and I don't even know who he is responsible to. One useful thing we learned from the Communists is the cell system. I know only Mr. Foxx and five other men in the organization. As far as I'm concerned they are the organization. They may well be, or there might be hundreds of us." Archibald, who smiled a lot without seeming to mean it, smiled again. "For all I know we are run by the Scouts of America, but that, by God, is security. What you don't know, you can't tell. Right now you know more than you should, which is unfortunate . . . for us and for you." He rang the elevator bell. "By the way, there is a little thing called the Espionage Act which is full of dire threats. What has and will transpire is covered by it. In plain language, keep your mouth shut."

Hardy had the car drop him in front of the Baskin-Robbins on Amsterdam Avenue. Armed with a German chocolate cake ice cream cone he munched his way home. He took Holmes for a perfunctory nervous walk and fastened all the locks when they got back to the apartment.

After a quick grilled ham and cheese, he set about preparing dinner. While he worked, he thought. He had to call those lawyers again: He pounded the veal and imagined it was Foxx and Archibald and Brown Suit—and Alice Henry for getting him into this mess.

Flour. Salt and pepper. Butter. Marsala wine. Bouillon.

He left the assembled ingredients and went into his office and started his list.

1. Walter Henry killed in unknown way on military installation (?post)

2. U.S. gov't interested but won't say why . . . or anything else.

3. Other people interested. Dangerous people.

4. One gov't agent dead (killed by Brown Suit?).

And that was it. It wasn't much of a list, but that was all he knew. He pinned it to the cork wall next to his desk and went back to the kitchen.

He took some ground chuck out of the freezer for Holmes and dredged the veal in the flour and salt and pepper.

His mind wasn't on what he was doing. He put the floured veal and the butter back in the refrigerator and headed for his barber chair and the TV. Even Errol Flynn in *Gentleman Jim* couldn't keep his at-

47

tention. He left the TV on and took a tranquilizer and wrote a new list.

THINGS TO DO

1. Call lawyers and get bio on Walter Henry, including jelly business.

2. Go to jelly factory in New Jersey.

3. Check recent newspapers at library or N.Y. *Times* for story about Walter Henry's death . . . if any.

4. Find out who he knew and talk to them.

5. Look over effects in apartment and office at jelly factory and N.Y. office (if there is one).

He pinned this list next to the other. He knew he should get started on it right away, but since it was Saturday . . .

After Flynn took the title from Ward Bond and kissed Alexis Smith, Hardy turned off the set and finished making his veal scaloppine alla marsala.

As a concession to Merle Doyle he ate it with spaghetti minus the garlic butter sauce. He also told himself the little salt he had used wouldn't hurt.

He spent the rest of the evening sipping Irish Mist brandy and watching the tube.

Sunday morning was spent reading portions of different books by Kazantzakis.

In the afternoon while some clever disc jockey was entertaining him by playing an old Henry Morgan routine about making a phone call from New England to California, the phone rang. It was Alice Henry.

"Hello, Pat, I thought I'd call to see if there was any progress."

"None to speak of, Alice, but I think tomorrow might be a little better."

"Pat . . . You have a lead. Wonderful. Tell me."

He made a face at the phone. "I don't want to say until I'm sure. . . . Alice, this is liable to get expensive."

"I don't care."

"I'm glad you feel that way. You see, I'm running short of working cash and I . . ."

She laughed. "No need to get embarrassed, Pat. That's sweet, a detective who gets embarrassed. I bet you're blushing. You are about the biggest hick I ever met. A New York hick. I'll put a check in the mail today. Pat?"

"What?"

"I received a strange letter yesterday. It was from Travis Corners. This old man, Jed Dorsey, he was a friend of my Aunt Jessie and he still does odd jobs around the courthouse. He said a man . . . an easterner or a foreigner, he couldn't tell which, was asking questions about me and my father and my Uncle Walter and could he see the records."

"And—"

"He didn't know the and. That's all he heard. He guesses the man was able to see the records, but he didn't know for sure. He didn't know what it was all about, but he thought I should know. Pat, does this have anything to do with my uncle's death?"

"It would seem that way, Alice. When did this all happen?"

"Four days ago. The only records he would find are

49

my birth certificate and my parents' death certificates. They weren't even married in Travis Corners. They were married in Dallas."

"Your friend, Mr. Dorsey, did he say what the stranger looked like?"

"No."

"Did he tell him about Dallas?"

"No, I don't think anybody ever knew my folks were from there."

"Do me a favor and tell him to cooperate with a fellow I'm going to send to see him. OK?"

"OK? What's it all about?"

"Maybe if I knew I could wrap this case up right now."

"Pat?"

"Yes."

"Do you remember what I said last time?"

Since he didn't break the silence, she did. "I said I missed you. I meant it."

"Honey, do you remember what I said to you the first day we met? I said that I wanted to get to know you better but that I did not like murder cases. Well, I'm involved in a murder case much against my own better judgment. I don't like it, and the things that are happening make me nervous . . . ."

"Pat! What things?"

"Never mind. It will all be in my report when and if I finish this case, but until that happens let's keep it simple, OK?"

"OK. But I still miss you and I'm coming to New

York as soon as I can get away from the store. Take care. Bye."

"Wait a minute. Call your lawyers tomorrow and tell them it's all right to talk to me and it's all right for me to get into your uncle's apartment and things like that. . . . I miss you, too."

He hung up on the lie before she could answer and slumped in his chair, suddenly very tired. He appeased his stomach with a Gelusil and drank a glass of cranberry juice. Then he made two phone calls. One to Ruby in Toronto telling her he couldn't make it. She wasn't too happy about that and neither was he. He hung up again and took another Gelusil and a tranquilizer. His second call was to Steve Macker, a many-talented friend who was working on a TV movie in Phoenix.

"Hello, actor."

"Pat, you son of a bitch. How are you and why are you calling?"

"I'm fine. How much longer do you have to work on that film?"

"As a matter of fact, we wrapped two days ago. I am in the midst of discovering what a fine town Phoenix is and I plan to spend all my money here and either head for L.A. or back to New York. I haven't made up my mind yet."

"Well, I just made it up for you. If you would care to do a little detective work for me, I would like you to go to Texas."

"And miss all the joys of Phoenix?"

51

"Stop the crap, Steve, you'll get a good price, and besides I hear the girls in Dallas aren't bad either."

"For how much?"

Pat talked money with Steve and then told him what he wanted him to do in Texas. When he was through he wrote Alice's new information on the first list and went back to his disc jockey friend who was now devoting his time to playing songs by Rodgers and Hart.

Chapter Five

On Monday after his workout and breakfast, he decided he would do better by going to see Messrs. Allenberg, Edgarton and Black rather than calling them. He never got there.

Annette de Montespan was the most exquisite woman he had ever seen. The blue-tinted monocle she affected seemed to make her more feminine rather than the reverse. Her car pulled into the bus stop in front of Hardy's apartment just as he was closing the outside door. It wasn't a Mercedes, but the man driving it was Brown Suit who was now wearing a gray suit. Nevertheless, when this exotic blond asked him to get into the opulent-looking black Lincoln, Hardy barely hesitated. She introduced herself. Then she said, "And I believe you have seen Joseph from time to time. Patrick Hardy, this is my very good friend and associate, Joseph Korboff. The studio, Joseph."

"Yes, Duchess."

"Well, 'Duchess,' what's this all about?"

"The title is not obligatory, Mr. Hardy. In fact, many people claim I have no right to it anymore, but Joseph's family and mine go back for generations. You may call me Annette."

"Thank you, Annette, but it fits you, if anyone ever looked like a duchess you do. What's this all about, Duchess?"

She seemed pleased by his remark. "An American who knows how to be gallant. . . . I didn't know there were any."

She pressed a button and revealed a portable bar. She opened a box and took out a small Danish cigar. "May I offer you something?" Her nails were violet.

Hardy shook his head, and not wanting her to think his gallantry was a sometime thing, he lit her cigar. She sighed some smoke out and looked at him for a long moment. "Mr. Hardy, I would like to hire you to investigate the death of a man named Walter Henry."

Hardy kept his mouth shut and thought. It seemed obvious that she knew he was working for Alice Henry and why. She might even know about Foxx and Archibald, if not exactly who they were. Since honesty was the best basis for a lie, he told the truth. "I'm already working for someone on that same case. To be quite honest . . ." And here the lie came: ". . . I think it's hopeless and after I check out a few more

54

angles, I'm going to tell my client that and drop the whole matter."

"That's just the point, I don't want you to drop the matter. I have no objection to your continuing to work for Miss Henry. In this day and age a person must make his money where he can. All I ask is that you let me know what you let her know. It can be very profitable . . . and more so."

In spite of everything else, visions of more money and the duchess' unclothed body flickered in his mind. His lips were very dry. "Why are you interested?"

The duchess snuffed out her cigar. "Ah, here we are. Why don't you come in and watch me work while you think it over?"

The studio was quartered in a private four-story house in the rich East 80s.

Hardy's eye darted toward Joseph Korboff and wondered how much of a threat was implied.

"Oh my," said the duchess, "don't think such sinister thoughts. I have my own photography studio and I run a modeling agency. I merely thought you might like to think about my offer in pleasant surroundings. If you would rather not, Joseph will drop you where you wish to go and you can call me when you've made up your mind."

Her almost violet eyes started chemical juices flowing inside him and he was intrigued by that monocle. So much so that the Walter Henry case and its ramifications had nothing to do with what he was thinking. "Duchess, it will be my pleasure."

As they got out of the car, he wasn't sure but he thought he heard her murmur, "And mine too."

A very bull-dykey-looking woman opened the door and let them in. She beamed at the duchess and sneered at Hardy. Korboff had gone off to park the car. Hardy was led past the entrance to the kitchen and past the staircase to the upper floors and through a large room that seemed to double as a study and a photography studio. One side of the room was open space and had a large white drop covering the wall. The other side had a large desk and chair that was flanked by settees and arm chairs. The walls were obliterated equally by unfathomable surrealistic paintings and photos. What interested Hardy most was that some of the photos were of nudes. He wasn't allowed to linger though. The duchess sat at the desk and nodded to the dyke who led him outside to a well-kept and well-fenced garden.

"I am Claude," she announced in an accent he couldn't place. "Do you want anything to drink? . . . to eat?"

"No, thank you."

She almost sneered again. Then after a moment of the two of them standing and not saying anything, she strode back into the house. She was built like a truck driver. Even so Hardy wondered what it would be like to make it with a dyke. He nearly stumbled over a large turtle. It took him a second to realize the monstrosity was not alive but made of metal. He instinctively checked his trick left knee and then stood on his left leg and did several bending exercises. When he was through he embarrassedly looked around to see if anyone had seen him.

Despite the heat of the day, the garden was comfortable. He admired the roses and other flowers he couldn't name and sat down on a lawn chair and wondered what the hell he was doing there when the duchess came out.

"Sorry, there was some business I had to attend to. Would you like to stay for lunch?"

"Sure."

"I'm afraid you'll have to excuse me again though. I have a picture session and I have to go upstairs to change. There's whiskey and cheese inside. . . . Claude, come and help me change."

This last was called out as she went upstairs and as Hardy sauntered back into the studio. He spread some Boursin cheese on a square of black bread and watched the butch follow the duchess. He wondered where Korboff was. After checking the hall, he went to the desk. All the drawers were locked but one of the papers on top seemed to be a schedule of appointments for people at such and such photographer or such and such ad agency. He took it to be a booking sheet for models. What struck him was that most of the bookings seemed to be at one agency more than others. And that he had heard of the others, but not this one. He made a mental note of Raven, Thompson and Peck with the thought of adding it to the second list on his cork wall.

His tongue reminded him how good the garlic-flavored cheese tasted. He went back for more and mixed himself a scotch and soda. It was early for him to be drinking but he was enjoying the situation. Looks at some of the nudes made him horny. Looks behind them told him that the duchess had taken them. Behind the terrible paintings he found dust and the names of the gallery they all came from and the man who did the framing. He would add Ludwig Lerche and Eddie Taylor to his list of people to see.

He was on his third trip to the cheese board when Korboff came in and started pulling strobes and lamps out of a closet and setting them up.

The duchess, now dressed in slacks and a man's shirt, came down followed by Claude just as the doorbell rang. Claude went to the door.

The Swedish type she admitted was one of the women whose nude pictures Hardy had seen on the wall.

Solveig Jensen was introduced to Hardy and then sat primly, waiting to be told what to do. The next ring admitted Gerrie Hayes and Mee-ling Lee. Hardy tried to keep his ogling down to a sophisticated minimum. The black model was attractive but Mee-ling took his breath away. He never knew that Chinese women could have such full breasts. Unfortunately, there were no nudes of Gerrie or Mee-ling on the wall.

After the duchess introduced the newcomers she said, "It's too close to lunch to start. We'll eat first and then we'll work."

The girls all nodded and Hardy followed suit. When

they reached the first floor, the dining table was all set up.

Endive salad. Quiche Lorraine. Cold Chablis. Breasts to the left of him, breasts to the right of him. And the duchess' monocle, twinkling and emphasizing those eyes, and that face. Hardy was in heaven.

Not quite. When he looked in the wrong direction there was always Korboff and Claude watching him. He wondered which would be more dangerous to fight . . . and he didn't want to find out.

After lunch Korboff disappeared and the rest of them went back downstairs. The models entered a side room off the hall and the duchess instructed Claude how she wanted the lights set. Hardy sat and waited, not knowing what else to do. He was intent on watching the duchess loading her camera. He was about to ask what kind it was when the girls traipsed in.

The abundance of nude flesh was breathtaking, and the contrast of skin tones made everything even more erotic. Hardy didn't know where to look first. That tell-tale part of his anatomy was reacting. And . . . he was sweating.

Everyone else in the room ignored him. This partially relieved and partially annoyed him. Nevertheless, he watched with great interest.

Regardless of their nudity, the first thing that caught his attention was their hair. Solveig's slightly wavy blond hair hung past her breasts as did Mee-ling's straight black hair. Gerrie's natural stopped at her shoulders, where it flared out.

Solveig's and Mee-ling's breasts peeked at him

59

through tresses of billowing hair as they moved, while Gerrie's, out in the open, stared straight at him.

All three were well endowed but Mee-ling's breasts were by far the largest and firmest. And Hardy had a thing about breasts.

Without losing sight of those beautiful nippled things he dropped his eyes lower. Flat stomachs, except for Gerrie who had a slight tantalizing curve. Full womanly hips. Mee-ling had almost no pubic hair at all. The other two had an abundance that agreed with their coloring.

Satisfied with their legs, he wanted to see their behinds. As if by design the duchess had them turn and walk toward the backdrop.

The first imperfection. Mee-ling had a birthmark the size of a quarter on her left cheek. Still, it was a lovely display. The duchess was now posing the girls with their arms reaching skyward.

Hardy was no longer examining each girl individually. Gestalt voyeurism was definitely in. As their bodies moved this way and that so did his eyes.

Hardy didn't know what to expect and didn't care. He watched the duchess pose the girls individually and paired and trioed.

A part of his mind dwelt on a fantasy orgy when they were finished, but when the session was over the duchess thanked them and dismissed them along with Claude and sat down at her desk.

Hardy fidgeted and coughed.

The duchess didn't look up from her paperwork but said, "I'll be with you in a moment."

When she did look up he said, "And what was that all supposed to be about?"

The monocle twinkled. "Nothing, just me doing my work."

He started to say something, realized it made no sense at all and let it dribble into a soundless mumble.

She smiled at him. "What was that? Never mind. Now we come to your work. As I said before, I would like to hire you to investigate the death of Mr. Walter Henry. . . . I know you have already been hired to find out who killed him. That is of secondary importance to me. What I want to know is: Who was Walter Henry? Why was he killed? And then, who killed him? This in no way should interfere with the arrangements you have made with Alice Henry. And, I will give you ten thousand dollars in cash as a retainer and twenty thousand more when the job has been completed. Good. Dreary business is now over. How boring it can get to be sometimes. Let's go upstairs to bed. I found those young girls' bodies quite stimulating, and I noticed you weren't bored by them either." She kept this banter going as they climbed the stairs to the third floor. "You may have thought I was a lesbian, actually I'm bisexual. Any good-looking naked body can arouse me."

They were in a large bedroom with mirrored walls and ceilings.

"I like the mirrors because even my own body arouses me. The thought of your body arouses me. Get undressed."

Like a soldier obeying orders he started to strip.

She caressed his biceps and chest. "Very nice. Very nice indeed. You're getting thick in the waist but otherwise, good. Now you watch me," and she removed the shirt she wore and preened at herself in the mirror. "Aren't I as sweet and firm as those young girls?" She dropped her slacks to the floor and kicked off her shoes. Completely nude she moved toward him, always watching herself in the mirror. Still watching, she undid his pants and knelt down in front of him.

Three hours later she was in ecstasy and he rolled over, frustrated and exhausted. For the first time in his life, he hadn't had an orgasm. Why?

She was smoking one of her Danish cigars and serving him Grand Marnier in milk and babbling about how marvelous he was, "Darling, you are the best. Even better than a young Russian I once had, K.G.B. But he went through training . . . doing multiplication tables in his head and such. All technical But you are a natural lover . . . I hope you weren't doing multiplication tables while you were making love to me."

He shook his head and drank his milk.

"Good. Sleep and when you are awake we will do it some more."

The last thing he thought of as he drifted off was that she was still wearing that monocle.

It seemed like only minutes later that she was at him again. After another bout he got dressed and went home. Besides being terribly tired and confused, he was ten thousand dollars richer.

Chapter Six

It was late. Hardy noticed that the street light on his corner which had been out for two months was still out. He apologized to Holmes and fed him. Weary and discombobulated, he washed a tranquilizer down with orange juice and took the ten thousand dollars out of his pocket. He sat down and sipped the juice and stared at the money. He put the money and the glass on the table and picked up the book that was lying there. It was *Thurber Carnival.* He thumbed through it absent-mindedly while he worried about his inability to have an orgasm. Too distracted to read, he looked at the sequence of drawings in "The War Between Men and Women."

He closed his eyes for a moment.

He opened his eyes and saw the daylight through

the windows and looked at his watch. Seven A.M. He had slept the night through in the chair. He picked up Thurber and put him down and picked up the money and placed it in the wall safe behind the George Grosz drawing.

As he paced around the apartment, he tried to review what had happened the day before, but his mind kept coming back to one thing. He hadn't had an orgasm.

He shaved and showered and tried to go back to sleep. Sleep wouldn't come. He soaked two rectangles of shredded wheat in milk and spooned them down and went into his office. He took the THINGS TO DO list from the cork wall and added:

6. Check out Raven, Thompson and Peck Advertising Agency.

7. Ditto Ludwig Lerche Gallery.

8. Ditto Eddie Taylor (Framer).

He was about to pin the list back on the wall when the thought came to him:

9. Mee-ling Lee.

Hardy looked at his watch. It was too early to call Merle Doyle. He considered calling another doctor. The thought of telling Merle about his new ailment distressed him.

He called the proper city number and complained about the nonfunctioning street lamp.

He got up from his desk and browsed through his old record albums. After placing Benny Goodman, Carmen McRae and Dave Brubeck, "Follies" and

George Gershwin on the phonograph, he stretched out on the barber chair and tried to relax.

Holmes barking at Laura's entrance woke him. "Morning," she said.

He grunted and lay there thinking only of the music and nothing else.

"Mr. Hardy, I hate to bother you, but something's got to be done about that kitchen sink, it's still leaking."

"I'll take care of it, Laura." He got up and splashed his face and got dressed. Remembering what he was trying to forget, he called Merle Doyle's office.

"Merle, I know my appointment isn't till next week but I have to see you."

"All right, Pat, come on over and I'll squeeze you in."

He went into the super's office and told him about the sink and then started the three-block walk to Merle Doyle's office. He stopped to examine some new graffiti advertising the macho-ness of the "Latin Kings" on the brick wall of a building, when he noticed a woman allowing her dog to use the sidewalk as a toilet. "Lady, would you please take your dog into the gutter?"

"Why don't you mind your business?"

"It is my business, I happen to live in this city."

The dog was finished. The woman snorted at Hardy. "I don't give a shit."

"Look again, lady, you just did."

They stared at each other and then Hardy walked away in disgust.

He knew his pressure was up. He walked past Merle Doyle's office for several blocks. When he thought he was calm, he doubled back on himself.

"I've got news for you, Patrick, your pressure is fractionally lower than it was the last time."

This was news. He thought the past events plus the incident with the woman and the dog would help him make a new blood pressure record.

"What else is troubling you?"

"Uh . . ." He didn't know how to say it. "Well, yesterday, I . . . This woman and I . . . We were in bed together and I couldn't make it."

"You mean you couldn't function?"

"No. I could function all right. I just couldn't make it. First time in my life."

Merle tried not to laugh. "Don't look so tragic. It's probably the tranquilizers. Keep taking them for your hypertension, but stop if you plan a little roll in the hay, they're relaxing you when you don't want to be. Forget about next week's appointment."

"Is that it?" he said incredulously.

"Well, if you want to hedge your bet, you might take some vitamin E everyday. . . . But knowing you, I think it would be gilding the lily. If what they claim about it is true."

He left to the strains of Stravinsky and walked up Broadway to the drugstore.

He felt better now and looked at the world around him. The hookers and junkies were out, but they didn't seem as ugly as usual. One nodder intrigued him. The man, who was well dressed and not at all crummy looking, was standing in front of a store window, seemingly window-shopping. Actually he was nodding as the result of whatever garbage was in his system. Hardy was fascinated with the way the man stood there nodding off to sleep, almost falling, and then snapping back to nod some more. Hardy didn't leave till the nodder snapped fully awake enough to walk away.

"What'll it be, Pat?" asked Hank Bianco.

"Give me some vitamin E."

"Got a heavy date?"

"Hank, you are the funniest druggist I know . . . and I don't know any funny druggists."

The handymen were still making noises in his kitchen so Hardy took Holmes for a walk. He took the jar of vitamin E capsules with him and Adele Davis' book on keeping fit.

Holmes wandered in the grass and Hardy read. He could find no mention of vitamin E making a person sexier, despite the rumors that had been going around, but he did find that it seemed to help people with high blood pressure. A little rumor, a little fact. He would try it.

Back in the apartment he gave the departing handymen each a beer and stole some of Holmes' ground chuck for a hamburger. After eating he took a vitamin E and thought about a tranquilizer, but skipped it. While he drank a glass of ginger ale he tried to clean up the burnt frying pan. After fruitless scraping he left it soaking in cream of tartar dissolved in hot water. Laura looked at the pan and at her employer.

67

She said nothing but scrubbed the pan clean with steel wool.

He mixed a scoop of vanilla fudge ice cream with black cherry jello and walked into his office to stare at Mee-ling's name on his second list.

Laura's leaving interrupted his musing. Like it or not, it was time to go to work.

He visited the lawyers' office to get filled in on who Walter Henry was. Not only were the lawyers typical of their breed—many words and few facts—but the girls in the office were ugly.

Next stop, New Jersey, where he met Frank Novick, the General Manager of Henry's Dietetic Jelly Company. He got the grand tour and learned how jelly was made and that Walter Henry was an absentee boss who was easy to work for.

Then a trip to Henry's apartment. Hardy walked through it and made a casual search, certain as he did that there was nothing to be found.

Walter Henry's New York office had been rented again. Nothing there.

Hardy rechecked his list and made notes on the results. Items 1, 2, 4, and 5:

1. Walter Henry was born, he lived and he died.

2. Except for the General Manager of Henry's Dietetic Jelly Company, the workers there knew nothing about him. And what the General Manager knew wasn't much.

4. If W. H. had any friends they were keeping low profiles.

5. To the workers and neighbors at Walter Henry's

New York apartment and office he was just another tenant. They saw him come and go, but didn't remember much about him.

Typical of New Yorkers, Hardy thought.

He had saved the dullest job for last. First he stopped on 42nd Street for a hot dog and a root beer and then another hot dog. Sated for a while, he meandered over to where the New York *Times* stored old news.

Item 3 was a different thing. A back issue had a small story tucked away about an unidentified dead man, who had been shot, and whose body had washed up on Fire Island. There were no further stories about the incident.

It was the following Tuesday by the time he came up with that little gem. Wednesday found him on the 9:10 to Bayshore. At 10:34, just minutes after the train had stopped, a hustling limousine driver rushed Hardy and other Fire Island-goers to the ferry. The ferry took him to the area near where the body was reported. The lone policeman in the one-room police station didn't help at all, except to tell him where the body had washed up.

No cars were allowed on the island and it took some doing for Hardy to hire a bike. He rode to the spot on the beach the policeman had told him about and stared out at the water. He considered and rejected the idea of renting a boat in one thought.

Hardy caught the 5:28 back to New York. By 7:30 he was in his own apartment eating his own concoction of shrimp and lemon-butter sauce and rice and green peas.

Tomorrow he would have to visit item 6 on the list: the Raven, Thompson and Peck Advertising Agency. Meanwhile, *Sitting Pretty* and *Singin' in the Rain* were scheduled that night on the tube. Hardy made himself a batch of Akvavit Bloody Marys and opened a can of paté and settled in for an enjoyable evening.

In the morning after his workout and breakfast he went to the library and checked the maps of the area surrounding Fire Island.

When he came back Laura told him the phone had rung several times. A check with his service told him that Alice had called from Texas, and Ruby had called from Toronto. He decided to call them both that night, and took a cab to lower Madison Avenue and the offices of Raven, Thompson and Peck. As he was going in, Mee-ling was going out.

They exchanged hellos, and he invited her for coffee. She accepted. Before he left her he found out she preferred to be called by her American name, Linda, and invited her for dinner at his apartment that night. She accepted.

As he was reentering the building, it occurred to him that he had been getting a little careless. He walked out a side door and back in through the front. Satisfied that he wasn't being followed by either Korboff or any of Foxx's men, he went upstairs.

The receptionist looked up from her paperback. "Yes?"

"Excuse me, could you tell me who your casting director is?"

"Leave your picture and resumé." And she was back to her book.

"No, you don't understand, I'm not an actor or a model or anything like that, I'm just a salesman, but people keep telling me I'm the right sort of person for commercials and . . ."

He purposely let the sentence dribble away.

She looked back at him and inspected him critically. "You might be right. Her name is Rickie Shirley. Call her and ask for an appointment."

"Oh . . . Well, you see, I'm on my lunch hour . . ." And here he gave her his best "little boy" shy smile.

"All right, I'll see if she can see you."

Rickie Shirley peered at him through granny glasses and asked him to sit down. "Now, Mr. . . . ?"

"Easy, Mike Easy."

"Well, Mr. Easy, I understand you want to do commercials."

"Yes, I know it takes a lot of training, and I never acted or anything like that but . . ."

"As a matter of fact, you're quite right. You could be a model or even an actor, but the first thing you need is pictures. The second thing you need is an agent. I'll give you someone to go to see who can help you out on both counts." She scribbled something on a piece of paper. "Good luck."

And he was out of her office and into the hall. He pushed the down button and was about to unfold the paper she had given him when he saw Solveig Jensen coming out of an arriving elevator. Hardy turned his back. It wouldn't do for too many people to see him here. He heard her ask the receptionist for Rickie Shirley as the down elevator he was waiting for opened its doors. In the elevator he read what the casting director had written. It was the name and address and phone number of Annette de Montespan.

He wasn't surprised, but he felt like a dog chasing its own tail. From the duchess to Raven, Thompson and Peck, and back to the duchess. Well, at least he had tonight with Mee-ling to look forward to. He hailed a cab and gave the driver his Riverside Drive address. While he rode he planned what he would have for dinner that night. Then a thought intruded and he had the driver drop him at the 53rd Street library instead. In the reference room he found a book which told which ad agencies handled which accounts for the various companies across the country. The firm Raven, Thompson and Peck was barely mentioned . . . and yet it had a whole floor of a building and seemed to have a great many people on its staff.

Hardy walked up to Central Park where he bought a taco from a street vendor. He strolled the rest of the way through the park and then west, trying to get little pieces of unrelated information to come together. On Broadway he stopped long enough to pick up several chicken breasts and the *Post* and went home.

Remembering not to take a tranquilizer, he read the paper and then grabbed two books at random from his shelf. He read the forward to *Ulysses* and decided that he wasn't in the mood for James Joyce.

The other book was a present someone had given him several years back that he had never gotten around to reading. An hour later he had finished *84, Charing Cross Road* and was sorry he had waited so long to read such a charming book.

TV Guide had nothing for him at the moment, but it did schedule *The Man Who Never Was* for later that night. It must be Clifton Webb week, he thought. Then his mind got involved in the logistics of enjoying the pleasures of dinner and Mee-ling and the movie without one infringing on the other. He thought about it while he folded the chicken around the butter and chives. After rolling and dipping and rolling again he put then into the refrigerator and added various spices to a large can of peaches and put that on the stove to simmer.

When his pre-preparations were done he checked the apartment to see if everything was neat and orderly. As a precaution he took both lists from the cork wall and placed them in his desk. He fed Holmes early and went into the bathroom to shower and shave.

By the time the doorbell rang Hardy had changed his shirt three times. He looked out at the street through the TV viewer. God, she was beautiful. With Holmes at his heels he went to the front door to let her in.

"Hi."

"Hi. Come on in. Holmes, get the hell out of the way. Go ahead. Inside. Inside."

"Oh, what a lovely apartment," she said. "Do you mind if I look around?"

"Be my guest. What do you drink?"

"Anything."

While she wandered he poured two scotches on the rocks and put some now sounds on the phonograph which he didn't care for, but thought would please her.

"A gym. Your own private gym! That's what I call living."

He handed her her drink. "You don't want too much out of life."

She sipped her drink. "It's beautiful."

"You're not kidding?"

"No, I'm not. I know, as far as you're concerned I'm just a model and I pose for pictures and do a few commercials. But I'm more than that."

"I know."

"Please don't be that way. I thought you were different. I'm a dancer and a good one. I also happen to be a very good gymnast."

They wandered back into the living room. She put her drink down and looked over his collection of pictures and paintings.

"These are good. Are you a gymnast?"

"No. I just use the gym to keep me in shape, but fancy stuff on the parallels and the high bar are beyond me."

She picked up her drink and smiled at him over the rim of the glass. "I could teach you."

He freshened her drink. "Amuse yourself while I

see about dinner. . . . Holmes, get away from that glass."

She smiled at the dog's antics. "May I come in and watch?"

"OK, but no kibitzing."

She watched silently while he fried the chicken, and readied the rest of the meal. Within a half hour he said, "Dinner is served. Scat. I'll bring it all out. That way if anything falls on the floor, I won't have anyone to blame."

"Yes, sir."

With the lights lowered and music sweetened, Hardy served chicken a la Kiev, spiced peaches and wild rice. They washed it down with Dom Perignon. Dessert was fresh strawberries and Cockbury port. They had spoken very little during the meal. While they drank their coffee and B. and B., she said, "That was absolutely the best. You sure have some technique. If that's what you do for openers, I can't wait to see what your second move is like."

He looked at her for a moment, then deliberately putting both hands on her luscious breasts, he kissed her. Then, just as deliberately, he broke the embrace and got up and turned on the TV. His timing was perfect, the movie had started only minutes before. He lay down on the chaise and beckoned to her with a nod of his head. She laughed out loud and joined him. Lying like two spoons they sipped brandy and smoked cigarettes and watched the movie. As Linda snuggled in tighter she said, "That's a great second move." The only problem was that she had nothing on under her dress. Her round bottom wiggling at his crotch and those erect nipples under his hands were too distracting. . . . So they missed the middle part of the movie. That was all right, Hardy had seen it before. When the picture was over she said, "I have an idea."

"Hm?"

"Let's go into the gym."

"What?"

"Let's go into the gym."

They had kept their clothes on during their movie intermission. Now as she ran into the gym Linda wriggled out of her dress and let it drop to the floor. When Hardy joined her she was hanging from the high bar, swinging back and forth. "Come on," she said, "get undressed and let's play." He watched in disbelief as she did a kip-up and sat on top of the bar. He flinched as her bare breasts rubbed on metal. "That must have smarted."

"It only hurts when I laugh," and then she leaned back and hung there by her knees. Hardy walked around and examined her from every interesting angle. Her long hair brushed the floor while her huge breasts seemed to defy the law of gravity.

"You like what you see?"

"Yes, Ma'am."

"Then let's play." And with that she did a neat drop to the floor and lay on the mat in a prone position, grinning up at him. She caught his eyes looking at the mark on her bottom. "My father said that's where the devil bit me."

"He must have had quite a sense of humor."

"Yeah, you wouldn't believe it if I told you."

"Try me."

She frowned and stuck her leg between his knees and knocked him to the mat beside her. "Now, Pat, now."

As they lay there in the sleepy haze that follows sex, she told him that her family had come from Kunming and that she had been born in Chicago. When he asked her more about her father, she changed the subject and they talked of other things, among them the different men she had dated, among them Joseph Korboff.

"Is he any good?" asked Hardy.

She pinched him hard. "His idea of making love to a woman is to imitate a jackhammer. Bang, bang, bang, bang. No finesse at all, not like some people I know." And she put her tongue in Hardy's ear. "He did teach me to skin-dive though. That was fun. But I don't like going out with him, he's got a cruel streak. Very creepy guy . . . Pat?"

"What?"

"We haven't tried the parallel bars yet, or the rings."

And then they did things no gymnast would ever had dreamt of.

In the morning they made it again. Then a duet workout in the gym and a shower together. After they cleared the dishes from the night before, she cooked them a large breakfast. They shared an after-breakfast cigarette and he and Holmes walked her to Broadway and put her in a cab.

Back in his apartment he patted the bottle of vitamin E capsules, planning to continue using them. In his office he dialed the phone. Ruby was no longer at her Toronto hotel and had left no forwarding address. He wondered how he would go about making it up with her as he dialed the number of the store where Alice worked in Houston. He was told she wasn't in that day.

He tried to think up an excuse for not returning her call sooner as he dialed her home number.

"Hello."

"Hi, Alice, it's me, Pat."

"Oh, hold on a minute. Steve," she said without moving her mouth away from the phone, "I think it's a friend of yours."

"What?"

"Hi, old buddy," said the familiar voice of Steve Macker.

"Don't 'old buddy' me, you double-crossing bastard."

"Good. I knew you wouldn't be sore."

There was some angry female noise after this that Hardy couldn't make out. When it stopped Steve was back on the line. "She sure has a temper, and is she mad at you."

"I thought you were in Travis Corners or Dallas. What are you doing in Houston? And what are you doing with Alice? Never mind, don't answer. Knowing the two of you I know what you've been doing—friend."

"Forget about all that. After I finished up in Dallas,

I figured it might be a good bet to check things out here too. When I showed up last night Alice was waiting for you to call. And what happened, happened. I'm pretty sure you'll do the same for me someday. Let's iron out our collective love lives another time. . . . Alice, where are you going? . . . Now she's mad at me, too. Never mind, it's just as well. I didn't tell her what I found out. She's your client, you tell her what you want to."

Hardy fumbled for a Marlboro. "All right, big mouth, talk."

And he did and Hardy listened.

When Macker finished his report, Hardy said, "I'll be a son of a bitch."

"Gee," said Macker, "You sure do make pithy remarks."

"Go to hell . . . Steve?"

"Yeah?"

"How mad is she? Is she just mad at me personally or is she mad enough to fire me?"

"Last night she was ready to fire you. But I talked her out of it. You might say I straightened everything out."

"I'll bet you did."

"Come off it, Pat. What's a woman between friends?"

Hardy laughed. "You can make pithy remarks, too. Thanks, Steve, I mean for the work. Good job. Give my best to Alice."

He hung up and took a tranquilizer and stretched

out on the chaise. Holmes joined him there and after a brief contest for body space Hardy fell asleep.

Not ten minutes later he snapped awake. He knew . . . or at least he thought he knew. He had the answer to the whole cockeyed mess. but it didn't do him any good.

After an hour of concentrated thinking, he moved to call Archibald but realized he didn't know how. Then he started to call Friday to tell him to have Archibald call him. Instead he re-dialed Alice's number. "Hello."

"Hello, Alice, it's Pat again. Is . . ."

"Oh, Pat, I'm so glad you called back. If you hadn't I was going to call you, I swear. I'll forgive you, if you forgive me."

"Alice, I forgive you. Is Steve still there?"

"Well . . ."

"Alice, no games. This is important. Important for you. I've got to talk to Steve."

"All right, wait a minute. Pat? Is everything still the way it was with us?"

"What? Oh sure, Alice. Exactly the same. Could I please talk to Steve?"

In less than a minute Macker picked up the phone. "What is it with you, Pat, you got telephonitis?"

"No, but I think I've got this thing figured and I need you to do a couple of things for me. I want you to go back to Dallas . . ."

"Wait a minute. This isn't just a trick to get me away from Houston and Alice? Talk about Territorial Imperative."

"Steve, this is really important."

"OK, she was ready to throw me out anyway. What do you want me to do?"

Hardy told him.

This time when he hung up he went to the safe behind the Grosz.

He opened it and touched the ten thousand dollars and grinned. Then he took out his passport and other personal records and took them into his office to look them over.

When he was satisfied he put all the papers back in the safe and wrote on his second list a reminder to revisit Walter Henry's apartment. He would do that tomorrow.

Lunch was several slices of pizza and a spinach pie washed down by a Coke in a Greek pizza parlor near Bloomingdale's. Several blocks further uptown was Lerche's Art Gallery.

"May I help you," said the smartly dressed woman.

"Is Mr. Lerche available?" He gave her one of his best smiles. The smile didn't seem to take. "He's busy at the moment. Perhaps I can help you. I'm Mr. Lerche's associate, Mrs. Hunter."

"How do you do? My name is Easy. At the moment I have a small collection of Expressionists: Grosz, Dix, Schiele, that group. But lately my eye seems to be attracted to the Surrealists, about whom unfortunately I'm very ignorant. A friend of mine, Annette de Montespan, suggested I drop by and see Mr. Lerche."

"Wait here a moment, please." He watched her

walk away. She had a nice figure but he didn't feel that she was getting his signal. While he waited he looked at the walls that were covered with paintings as unmeaningful as those he had seen at the duchess' house. He picked up Mrs. Hunter's nameplate from her desk. "Mrs. Sally Hunter." He was wondering how he would go about making such a woman when a black man walked toward him. "Mr. Easy."

"Yes."

"I am Ludwig Lerche."

Hardy's confusion must have shown on his face.

"I know," said the gallery owner, "it's a shock to expect a Teutonic and to meet a black man instead. Please relax, I'm quite used to it and take no offense. Now then, Mrs. Hunter said you were recommended by the Duchess de Montespan and were interested in expanding your artistic vistas. Quite right, too, the Expressionist School is definitely passé."

Hardy listened to the man's prattle for another five minutes and then, with a brochure of the gallery's artists, and a promise to come back, he made his escape.

His luck was no better on Second Avenue where Eddie Taylor had his framing shop.

He went home and fed and walked Holmes and snacked from what leftovers he could find in the refrigerator. There was nothing on TV and he didn't want company, and there was a good double feature in one of the local movie houses. He went.

One and a half pictures and a box of popcorn and

two Hershey bars and one root beer, and a tranquilizer, later, he headed home.

The street light on his corner still wasn't working so he didn't see the black limousine sitting in the bus stop until he was right on top of it.

He couldn't see the duchess or Korboff but the figure sitting in the back looked very much like Claude. In the front seat were two very large men.

He was scared. He was trying to figure out a course of action when Claude got out of the car. She looked in his direction and saw him. Hardy cursed her for having the eyes of a cat and himself for not moving out of sight. "Good evening, Mr. Hardy. The duchess would like to see you. Would you please get in the car."

"No, thank you."

She rapped on the window of the car and the two men got out. Thankfully they didn't work as a team. Number one moved in on him several paces ahead of number two. Hardy turned to run but his brain ran away instead and his reflexes took over. Kicking backward he placed his right heel square in the man's groin and put him completely out of action. Hardy then did a shoulder roll in the direction he was already moving to get out of the reach of number two. As he turned to face him the second man grabbed him in a bear hug. Hardy hammered at both kidneys and stomped on the man's instep. When his attacker's grip relaxed slightly, he freed one hand and was jabbing for the throat when Claude chopped him very neatly across the back of his neck. He could hear Holmes barking from inside the apartment.

Chapter Seven

A blue light glimmered in the distance. It came closer. "There, darling, this will make you feel better," the duchess said and handed him a glass. Hardy drank the mixture of milk and brandy.

"Thanks, Duchess, you're a princess. I got your invitation and came as fast as I could."

She puffed delicately on her Danish cigar. "I'm so happy you're able to keep your sense of humor at a time like this. . . . I'm afraid you're going to need it. It seems that you have been a very bad boy."

They were in the duchess' bedroom and Korboff and Claude were at the foot of the large bed he was lying in. Hardy's first thought was Gog and Magog. His second was how he was going to get out of this particular mess. Flash went his smile. "Duchess, will you please tell me what this is all about?"

"It's about your investigating me. That was not what you were hired to do. Please," she continued as he opened his mouth to speak, "don't even waste your breath in trying to deny it. I know you have more intelligence than that . . . though, for an intelligent man you do foolish things. Mr. Lerche called me, as did Mr. Taylor. Actually they were only thanking me for sending a prospective customer. I put that together with the new model Rickie Shirley said she thought might be calling me." She caressed his face. "Really, Pat, you should think of a less transparent alias. 'Mike Easy' indeed. . . . Did you think because I wasn't born in this country that I had never heard of the Pat and Mike jokes? Believe me, Pat, this is no joke. Or were you just playing a game? Well, it is no game either. . . . Joseph, Claude. Bring in Mario."

When the two had left on their errand the duchess sat on the bed and embraced Pat. "You know I adore you. Why do you put me in such a dilemma? If it were up to the two of them, you would be dead right now. Fortunately it is not up to them, but me." She kissed him, "Please, after this, no more jokes and games. Just do the job you were told to do. If you do it well, there will be many more jobs, which will mean a lot more money for you. And until you bore me there will be me. And I assure you, you don't bore me. You annoy me very much, but you don't bore me. I am fickle, and some day you shall, but at this moment you excite me more than any man I have ever known. Right now it's all I can do . . ."

The door opened and Korboff and Claude brought in a frightened-looking man. The duchess kept on talking, but her tone was much harsher. "This is Mario. He is a member of our organization. For reasons that do not concern you he is in the need of discipline. I think if you witness this discipline it will serve as an object lesson to you." She paused and her mouth formed a weird smile. "And perhaps as an entertainment for me." She motioned for Pat to move over, and after arranging the pillows, she helped Pat to sit up and then joined him on the bed. "Very well, my two darlings, begin."

Soundlessly, and almost gently, Korboff and Claude removed the cowering man's clothing. Then Claude took the man's arms and held them behind his back in a vise-like grip. Korboff moved in on him.

"Stop," said the duchess, "Let us make this as amusing as possible. . . . Strip." She squeezed Pat's hand and smiled at him while the two methodically did as they were told. Claude was almost as solidly built as Korboff, even her breasts seemed like enlarged pectoral muscles. There was an ice-cold sensation grabbing at Hardy's groin and belly.

It was more teasing than torture to begin with. Pinches and pokes that must have been more irritating than painful and certainly no tax on the strength of the two perpetrators.

At a point Claude released Mario and looked to the

duchess. The duchess nodded and squeezed Hardy's hand again.

Now Korboff held the man and Claude started in. Her teasing was meaner and more obscene.

Eventually the man started to weep.

"All right," the duchess said, "that's enough. Take him away and don't come back till I send for you. You see, Pat, there is no need to permanently injure the body or even the mind of someone to discipline him or even to extract information. The ego is a more vulnerable target. Taken further I've seen this form of humiliation break men who withstood physical pain and all sorts of so-called sophisticated brainwashing. It is the ego that is the weak point, especially the sexual ego."

By this time the trio had gone.

Gently she bit his shoulder and scratched at it with her violet nails. "I'm sure I have made my point, darling. But what was a warning to you was pure eroticism to me," and she kissed him, thrusting her tongue deep into his throat.

Despite what had happened and knowing how kinky she was, Hardy was aroused by her educated hands and mouth.

She let him sleep after they had made love. When he awoke Gog and Magog were at the foot of the bed again. "Get dressed," said Claude.

Hardy rubbed the sleep out of his eyes and scrambled into his clothes. When he was finished, Korboff silently led him down to the door and out into the street.

He approached Central Park with the perverse thought of walking through it, but the thought of some junkie's knife in his belly convinced him not to.

He walked downtown instead, hoping either to hail a cab or catch the 79th Street crosstown. He checked his watch and, considering the hour, doubted the feasibility of either plan.

"Out for your constitutional, Mr. Hardy?"

By this time George Archibald's voice was imprinted on his brain. He was glad to see the car, but not the man inside. "Oh boy," he said in an exaggerated sigh, "two winners in one night. Come on, junior G-men, let's get it over with."

As they drove to the building on 35th Street, Hardy ruminated about his own kinkyness in enjoying his most recent sex with the duchess, considering the circumstances that had led up to it.

The consideration he gave it was very slight. He lit a cigarette, took three drags and snuffed it out and closed his eyes and napped.

And he dreamed. About a girl named Peg. He was telling her how beautiful she was. Even in passion she was vain. She made her flat stomach flatter and thrust her high breasts higher. Silently and desperately their lips and hands and bodies explored. It was the best he had ever known. He dreamed about her, clutching at her beautiful body which had an ugly red hole in it.

Even as he watched her dying he thought about her in bed and how good her breasts felt in his hands.

It was the best he had ever known.

And his eyes opened. The car had pulled to a

stop. Surprisingly the dream hadn't upset him at all. "Are we here?"

"Just changing cars." And they did.

When they stopped again Archibald said, "Stay put, please. One of my men is checking things out."

Things checked out and they went up in the freight elevator. There was Mr. Foxx puffing on one of his cigars.

Hardy wondered if he thought he looked like Churchill. He was thinking of asking him when Foxx said, "Of all the idiotic men I have ever met you are the most overweening." He puffed harder at the cigar. "It goes beyond description. You are a plethora of idiocy."

"For something that goes beyond description you're doing very well."

"Bah. Shut up and sit down," said Foxx. "Do you want something to drink? Have you eaten?"

"As a matter of fact I could use a sandwich and a glass of milk."

Foxx nodded to Archibald who whispered to the man at the door while Foxx continued his harangue. "I told you to continue your investigation. I didn't tell you to become a bosom friend of the duchess."

"Cute play on words."

Foxx ignored his comment and started to go on but Hardy said, "Look, I'm doing what you told me to do. It so happens the duchess wants me to investigate the death of Walter Henry, too."

Foxx and Archibald exchanged glances. Hardy didn't know if they were knowing glances or merely glances. Foxx smoked, Archibald stood patiently and Hardy fidgeted. Soon the door was knocked on and opened and a tray with his sandwich and milk were brought in. Hardy bit into the sandwich. "Hey, you guys serve a great snack, a caviar and sliced egg sandwich. Why didn't I ever think of that?"

Foxx glared at him. "It would most probably taste better not being a sandwich. Will you now please try to explain what you think you are doing? . . . I mean with the duchess, and no lewd jokes, I am not in the mood."

Hardy drank his milk. "If you're so concerned about her and know where she is, why don't you collect her and her people and get it over with and get me out of this mess?"

"Not until we are ready. What is going on between you and that woman? . . . Besides sex. . . . The dossiers on both of you are very clear on that subject."

Hardy burped lightly into his fist and lit a cigarette. "Are you going to tell me what this whole thing is all about?"

"No."

A new question occurred to him. "Was there ever any evidence of someone searching Henry's apartment after he died?"

Foxx poured himself and Archibald glasses of Grand Marnier and motioned an offer to Hardy.

"No, thanks. It really doesn't matter whether you tell me anything or not. I think I'm beginning to figure it out for myself."

Foxx rolled the liqueur in his mouth, savored it

and swallowed. "Your conjectures don't really interest us, merely your actions."

A silence, then Hardy said, "Well, to begin with, the duchess is not that concerned with who killed Walter Henry. She's more concerned with who he was and why he was killed. . . . I think she has a fair suspicion of who he was. What she wants from me is confirmation. . . . Mr. Foxx, are you going to give me any help on this at all?"

"Go on."

"I think the duchess thinks Walter Henry was one of your agents. I also think she was right."

Another set of glances between Foxx and Archibald.

"And," said Hardy, "as long as she's pretty sure of this, the simplest thing would be for you to give me some proof of it. You might even tell me why he was killed, if you know why, and I can bluff her about who killed him. She really doesn't seem to care much about that. Then I could be through with her. In a little while I could do as you asked and tell Alice Henry I'm stuck and can't figure out who killed her uncle. Then the case would be unsolved but closed in my books and you would have me out of your hair and be able to go about your cockamamie cloak-and-dagger business."

No comment.

Hardy lit a new cigarette and looked around at the office, especially at the two racks of dresses. "It just occurred to me that you have a great sense of humor. A business in the garment center as a cover for the cloak-and-dagger business. Do you sell knives as a sideline?"

Foxx looked as if he had a bad taste in his mouth. "Mr. Hardy, would you wait out in the hall, please?"

Hardy shrugged and let the man at the door help him out. He nodded at the man on post in the hall but got no response.

Less than five minutes later Archibald came out. Hardy looked at him questioningly.

"It's late," said Archibald, "I'll have one of my men drive you up to the Port Authority Bus Terminal. I'm pretty sure you can get a cab from there."

"Gee," said Hardy. "We sure are getting security conscious."

Archibald didn't answer him.

Chapter Eight

He said a quick hello to Holmes and headed for the john. Caviar, eggs and milk was not something his stomach could handle during the wee small hours of the morning. He was in there long enough to re-read all of *Slaughterhouse Five*.

The phone woke him with a wrong number. The wrong number he'd been getting for years. He agreed with the woman that he was the supermarket and took her order. Feeling slightly better he tried to get back to sleep, but sleep wouldn't come. It was a beautiful day but his sinuses didn't think so. He rubbed the bridge of his nose to activate the sinus passages and get rid of the headache. His stomach wasn't in any great shape either.

The sinuses cleared and the bad feeling eased up a

bit, but by that time he had rubbed the skin on his nose raw.

No workout today, but thoughts of the gym reminded him of what he and Linda Lee had experienced in there.

His stomach barely accepted the half grapefruit and cup of coffee. This annoyed him. As long as he could eat, life was bearable, no matter what his problems. He took a long shower and lay down again. His nose hurt where he had rubbed it. He got up and put vaseline on the tender spots.

Being up had broken the inertia. He got dressed and leashed Holmes and out they went. Two hours of walking brought him further back into the world of the living.

On the way he bought a half dozen new books, a pair of sneakers and a new iron for Laura. Feeling much better, he also bought a quarter pound of Nova Scotia lox, cream cheese and several bagels at Zabar's.

After a real breakfast he established himself in the barber chair and picked up one of the new books.

That night they went back out only long enough to pick up the Sunday papers. The books and the papers and television and eating and not answering his phone made up his weekend, which he carried through Monday.

On Tuesday the need for discipline arose anew in him. After an extra strenuous workout, he jogged around the park, stopping only long enough to watch some kids playing basketball. Hardy shook his head in wonder. It was too hot for basketball.

In the apartment he shaved and showered and after breakfast got fully clothed and went straight to his desk. He added Macker's information to the first list and placed the two lists back on the cork wall. And he stared. He stared at the lists. He stared at the wall. He stared at his desk. He stared at his phone. He went so far as to rest his elbows on his knees and stare at the floor.

When the phone rang it was Steve Macker reporting that he had done what Hardy had asked.

"Great, Steve, bring it home, will you."

"Would you mind very much if I made a little stop-over in Houston first?"

"Yes, I would."

When the phone rang again it was Alice.

After a tedious repetition of their last conversation, he managed to hang up. He wished Ruby would call with an invitation to join her while she toured Spain or something.

Staring at the phone didn't make it ring again and since he had no calls to make, he went into the kitchen for lunch and then started preparing dinner. When the carbonnades a la flamande were in the oven he set the timer and forgot all about his plans for discipline and settled down to watch *The Music Man*.

Humming "Seventy-six Trombones" he stopped watching the six o'clock news long enough to remove the herbs from the casserole and put the finishing touches on the sauce.

He was about to put the potatoes on when the doorbell rang.

95

Steve Macker's ugly-handsome visage was beaming up at him when he looked through the TV viewer.

Hardy let him in. Macker dropped his bags in the hall and tossed a manila envelope on the chaise and poured himself a large portion of I.W. Harper. Holmes' nose perked up when he smelled the whiskey.

"You're just in time for dinner. Then we can look over what we've got," said Hardy and he started to light the fire under the potatoes.

"Oh, no, you don't," Macker answered. "None of your home-cooked concoctions, and no work either. I could have gone straight home, but I came here so you could take me out on the town, to coin a phrase. I want you to spend your money so I can have a good steak, lots of booze and maybe run across some female companionship. Let's go out and have some fun."

"But," Hardy sputtered and pointed to the casserole.

"Have it tomorrow. Stuff like that always tastes better the second day."

"Yeah, but every time I go out someplace with you I get into trouble and I have more than I can handle right now."

They were on their second drink and had just finished ordering their steaks when Hardy saw Sally Hunter with Gerrie Hayes. Both women saw him and nodded. Hardy sort of nodded as the waiter seated them at a table near theirs.

"I saw that, you sneaky son of a bitch. What are you trying to do, keep all the good stuff to yourself?

Let's go introduce me. I'll even let you have your pick."

"Steve, wait a minute. I'm in a bind. I've met both those women while working on this case."

"So?"

"The black one, Gerrie Hayes, knows me as Pat Hardy and the other one, Sally Hunter, thinks my name is Mike Easy."

"A minor problem," and Macker was on his feet. "Come on, I'll think of a solution while we walk over."

As Hardy trailed along he realized his problem was only one of embarrassment since he had fooled no one with the Mike Easy name anyway. Macker was already speaking. "Hello, ladies. Allow me to introduce myself. My name is Steve Macker. You of course know my friend Pat Hardy, alias Mike Easy. We would be delighted if you would be our guests for dinner."

Hardy couldn't believe it. They were smiling and nodding and moving over so that the men could sit down. If he ever tried an approach like that, it would fall like a wet noodle. Not only that, Macker was sitting next to the fantastic Gerrie Hayes while he was stuck with the icy Mrs. Sally Hunter whose eyes were already telegraphing the question about his contradiction in names.

While she asked the expected question, Macker signaled the waiter that they had moved and that he was to bring their order to the new table. Macker, who seemed to be able to concentrate on several things at once, said, "I'm afraid you'll have to accept Pat as he is, Sally, eccentricities and all. Once for a week he went around telling everyone his name was Cardinal Spellman, insisting that Cardinal was his first name."

The outrageous thing of it to Hardy was that she bought the stupid story and she and Gerrie were laughing at it as if it were the funniest joke in the world.

Hardy paid the very large check and caught up to them in time to find out that they were all going to Gerrie's place for a nightcap.

"Goddamned nigger lovers."

Hardy wanted to keep walking and pretend it never happened.

Not Steve Macker. Slowly and deliberately he herded the girls back into the restaurant foyer. Then, without saying a word, he turned and headed for the five foul mouths who had originated the remark. Hardy was right behind him. The mouths were busy laughing.

"What's so funny?" demanded Macker.

The apparent leader of the group yelled, "Hey, the nigger lover's a hero."

Macker didn't waste time on words after that. He faked a right at the leader and with the same motion sidestepped and took on the one next to him with a left hand just under the ear. Then, as his momentum carried him toward the other three, he rapped the leader in the ribs.

Macker's move left the leader face to face with Hardy who was still standing there with his arms at his side. The frustrated man cocked his right hand.

Frightened, Patrick Hardy retreated into the safety of his mind and his reflexive self took over. He stepped under the moving right hand and completed the damage Macker had started on the man's ribs. When he was down Hardy turned to help Macker who was taking on the remaining three and getting the worst of it. Moving in, Hardy gave an extra kick to the second neck of one of the three that Macker was dealing with.

Concentrated pressure for several seconds put that one away, and Hardy reached for one of the remaining two, but since Macker had finished one of them off there was only one left. In the state he was in Hardy couldn't check himself and he grabbed the man away from Macker's grasp like a kid taking another kid's toy. By this time the man was out. Hardy didn't care. He started to lift the man up in order to slam him to the ground when Macker grabbed him. Automatically Hardy tried to put his elbow through Macker's kidney but Macker avoided it. "Steady, Pat. It's over. It's all over."

Hardy's eyes cleared and he started to tremble. Macker held onto him and kept talking and he sat him down on the curb.

Satisfied that Hardy was all right and that there was no fight left in any of the five, Macker retrieved Gerrie and Sally who had stood in the doorway to watch and piled them all into a cab.

At Gerrie's apartment she poured them all large drinks and turned on some soft music and they all tried to think calm thoughts. Hardy's head had caught up with the rest of him and he was more or less composed. Sally had cleaned up several cuts and scrapes on his face and his body was sending out messages as to where he had been hit. He mentioned this and Macker shared his complaint.

"You know," said Macker, "you're right, I never seem to feel it while it's happening, but later on . . ." He drained his glass and refilled it. "How're you doing, tiger?"

Hardy grinned and raised his glass in a toast and drank.

After that they stopped talking about the fight. They drank and chatted until Macker let Hardy know, as subtly as he could, that he would appreciate if it he and Gerrie could be alone.

"It's getting late," said Hardy. "Come on, Sally, I'll take you home."

Gerrie lived in the East 50s, and Sally lived only a few blocks away. As they walked the liquor caught up with Hardy and he got drunker.

"If I were smart," said Mrs. Sally Hunter, "I'd put you in a cab and send you home, but you might not be able to find your door when you got there. Come on up and I'll give you some coffee."

"And sympathy. Coffee and sympathy."

Inside, a taste of coffee and he was out.

He awoke to find Sally in her robe watching TV and knitting.

"I hope that's a shroud you're knitting, Madame LaFarge. I could use one."

"Welcome back," and she got up and poured him fresh coffee.

"How long have I been out?"

"About an hour."

"What are you watching?"

"*All The King's Men*. Broderick Crawford is very good."

"He's a very good actor." Hardy turned so he could see the screen and they watched together. During the commercials he learned that she was still married.

"My husband has a travel agency in Zurich, but I prefer to live in New York. We visit each other quite regularly. It's not the average notion of a marriage but it suits us. It's what you might call a civilized arrangement. I like that word. Civilized. Yes, I am a civilized woman."

It seemed that somewhere between Gerrie's apartment and now, Sally had left and the icy Mrs. Hunter had returned.

The movie was over.

Hardy was trying to figure out whether to say good night and leave or to try to get beneath that icy exterior and that robe.

"Do you have any scotch?"

She stopped knitting. "Do you think you ought to?"

"Well," he said, walking behind her and placing his hand on her shoulder," I need something to protect me against the night air."

She snickered and started knitting again. "That remark wouldn't even sound good in the wintertime."

He placed his hand in that area between throat and bosom.

She kept knitting and said, "Don't you think you've exhibited enough masculinity for one night, Mr. Hardy? I said I was civilized, not promiscuous."

Completely frostbitten, he said good night and left.

He caught a cab almost immediately. Only after he got over his pique at being rejected did he even think it was a strange coincidence that Gerrie Hayes and Sally Hunter knew each other.

When he got home he added that to his first list and after drinking several glasses of water he went straight to bed.

It was well into the afternoon when Macker called to say that he was coming over.

Stumbling around, Hardy filled the electric coffee pot which he only used on special occasions, such as monumental hangovers.

Macker arrived grinning and whistling. "If you ball the way you fight, Pat old buddy, you made out like a maharaja."

Hardy stared at him. "Your eye's swollen."

"You're right, Pat, gentlemen just don't discuss those things. But I'm no gentleman, and let me tell you if you want to know what heaven is before you die . . ."

"Here's your coffee."

'Yes, sir," said Macker.

"And stop that whistling."

"Pal, if you're going to act like that the morning after then you have got to stop drinking."

102

"Now he tells me. I told you you would get me into trouble, and sure enough you did. My head hurts from too much scotch. My body aches from too many punches. My mind aches because I'm dumb enough to listen to you when you say, 'Let's go out and have a little fun.' I never learn. It always happens."

"Didn't get laid, huh? I thought you wouldn't. You don't have the right technique for that kind of woman."

"Shut up and drink your coffee. We have work to do."

"OK, but before we get started, could you fill me in on a few particulars?"

"OK," groaned Hardy, "but could you do me a favor?"

"Right, I'll stop whistling."

"Not that . . . That too. But, I'm starting to get hungry and if I look at a raw egg I'll get sick. Could you fry up a couple for me?"

"Sure. You talk and I'll cook."

While Macker made them some ham and eggs and more coffee Hardy disregarded Archibald's warning and told him about Foxx and the duchess, and swore him to secrecy.

"Who would I tell? Here, eat, look how bad you look."

When they were through eating and Hardy had lit up, he was beginning to feel almost human. "Thanks, Steve, you're a life saver. Let's get to work."

The manila envelope produced very little, but the contents pleased Hardy. He examined a copy of the birth certificate and the copy of the high school diploma. "How'd you manage to get these?"

"Trade secret," said Macker and grabbed one of Holmes' toys and played tug of war with the animal.

"Not enough," said Hardy. "Social Security card. College stuff. Army stuff."

Macker stopped fooling with Holmes and reached into his pocket. "I almost forgot. Couldn't get a copy of his Social Security card, but I did get a number." He handed Hardy a piece of paper. "He must have started working very young. What now?"

Holmes was now thrusting the pull toy at Hardy The animal saw that neither of his friends wanted to play and he walked away from them to find a place to sleep.

Hardy was thinking.

"Why not his lawyers?" Macker asked. "They must have some of his papers."

"One of three things," said Hardy, ignoring the suggestion. "We keep looking and collect more stuff. We take what we have and fake the rest. I figured with my passport and his picture and my college and Army records, we could mock-up some passable fakes. What would be better—photostats or an office copying machine?"

"Copying machine. And I know where we can get the use of one. Secretary I see once in a while whose boss is always out of town. But that's not too good an idea. What if you come up with a fake and the duchess has a real one that she's already dug up? She'll figure your whole package is worthless . . . and she'll be right. What's the third thing?"

"Walter Henry's apartment."

"I thought you searched it."

Hardy touched one of the tender spots on his face gingerly. "I just walked through it. I didn't know what I was looking for."

"You're trying to tell me something, Pat."

"Correct, wise-ass. I goofed off. I walked in, looked at each room, opened a drawer or two and convinced myself I had done a search job. Besides I was pretty sure others had been there before me. I'll get dressed and we'll go there now."

"Don't hurry. We've got plenty of time."

Hardy didn't answer him.

He still had the key for Walter Henry's apartment and the doorman on duty was the same one he met the last time.

Inside, the first thing Hardy did was take a photo of the late Walter Henry from its frame. "In case the only choice I have left is faking it, I can use it for the passport."

Macker shook his head. "I know I work for you, but I suggest we forget about plan two and concentrate on plan three."

Books came off shelves. Pictures were removed from walls. Three hours later they had found nothing.

"Funny," said Hardy, putting a pillow back in a chair and sitting on it.

"What?" asked Macker who was sitting on the floor.

"No safe."

105

"Lots of people don't have safes."

Hardy was up on his feet and examining the walls. "Not the Walter Henry I know. He would definitely have a safe, and a hidden one."

Macker rolled his eyes back and gave a fair imitation of Richard Burton. "Alas poor, Hardy. I knew him, Horatio." He switched to his own voice, "The next thing you know we'll be digging up the floors." And he started a burlesque tapping of the floors.

"You're a very funny man," said Hardy and continued his inspection of the walls.

A few minutes later he wondered why Macker was so quiet and turned around to find that his friend had rolled away a rug and was probing at the parquet with a knife. Hardy was about to comment when Macker lifted a two-by-three-foot section out of the floor. Macker reached in and said, "No safe. How does a strongbox grab you?"

He started working on the lock with his knife. "Patrick, I shall never doubt you again in my life."

Hardy grinned happily. "For a practiced thief you're sure taking a long time getting that thing opened."

Macker didn't look up. "Ex-thief, if you don't mind. Voila."

Voila indeed. Inside were Walter Henry's birth certificate. His high school diploma. His college diploma. Some R.O.T.C. papers. His Social Security card. His Army records. An expired passport. And some papers referring to the Henry Dietetic Jelly Company. And . . . three typewritten pages marked "TOP SECRET."

Hardy: "Talk about everything in one fell swoop."
Macker: "Looks too good to be true."

Hardy chewed his thumbnail. "They all must have been here before. Foxx . . . the duchess. It doesn't make any sense. A few conjectures."

"Be my guest."

"One," said Hardy, "they all missed it. Two, Foxx or someone else planted it here for reasons of their own. Two-A . . ."

Macker groaned.

"Two-A, maybe Foxx is helping me, but doesn't want me to know it. It would suit his plans."

"What the hell are his plans?" asked Macker.

"Sorry, buddy, I think I know, but I'm not even going to tell you that. . . . Well, at least they're trying to help me."

Macker wiped the empty strongbox with his handkerchief and set it back in place and covered everything up. "Not help . . . more like manipulate."

Chapter Nine

Hardy shared his carbonnades a la flamande with Macker and Macker reciprocated by sharing a bit of top quality hash with Hardy.

High and happy they sat there and listened to a bunch of "Memory Years" records.

They and Gene Kelly and Judy Garland and Artie Shaw and Fred Waring and Ted Weems and all the rest of those people had a very good time together.

And then it was the next day and Macker was calling him on the phone to see if his services were needed any longer.

"I'll tell you what, Steve, you play at being a detective and I'll play at being an actor. Even trade."

"No thanks, pal, I like things just the way they are.

If you're through with me, I'd like to get back to my personal life."

"Which I haven't interfered with too much," said Hardy. "No, I think I can blunder through the rest of this myself. I'll send you a check."

"Right. Later."

When Laura showed up, Hardy and Holmes went out into the park to think.

They came back as Laura was preparing to leave.

"The phone didn't ring, Mr. Hardy."

"Thank you."

"Why'd you buy a new iron?"

"I thought you could use it."

"Anything wrong with the way I'm doing your shirts?"

"No."

"Well, there's nothing wrong with the iron. What did you pay for the new one?"

"Goodbye, Laura."

"I bet they cheated you. What did you pay?"

"Have a nice weekend, Laura. See you next week."

"If I live until then," she said, and the door closed behind her.

"Me too," said Hardy to himself and mixed himself a batch of apple sauce and milk in the blender.

When he could think of no reason for putting it off any longer, he called Annette de Montespan.

After telling Korboff and then Claude that he would only speak to the duchess, she got on the line.

"Yes, my sweet boy."

"Do you have the twenty thousand dollars?"

109

"We seem to have a bad connection. Why don't you go outside and call me again on a pay phone?"

Hardy hung up and swore to himself that he would never see another James Bond movie again. These different factions and their hang-ups about bugged phones were getting on his nerves.

He went outside and remade the call.

"Darling Pat, I think you have good news for me."

"Do you have the money?"

"Don't be so mercenary, darling. Come to the house and if your merchandise is satisfactory you will be paid."

"Not the house."

"But then how can I give you your bonus?"

"I'll have to take a rain check on that. For today I think we should meet in what you people probably call a 'safe place.' "

"Darling, you are learning. I am truly impressed. Where?"

"The pay phone I'm calling you from is just a block north of where I live. Get in a cab and be in it in thirty minutes. I'll call you then."

"That is bizarre. Much too much. Caution is a good thing, but you've been seeing too many of those horrid spy movies."

"Thirty minutes, Duchess, and come alone." As he hung up he himself tended to believe that he was perhaps overdoing it.

He went back to the apartment and collected the material with the exception of those pages marked "TOP SECRET," and then went to Hank Bianco's drugstore and killed time talking to the druggist until the thirty minutes had passed.

He dialed the phone booth number. "Yes."

"Duchess, walk down to Lincoln Center and wait by the fountain. If you've been a good girl, I'll meet you there."

"This is ridiculous."

"I agree."

Hardy was about to leave the store when he spotted Hank's delivery boy putting some packages on the shelves.

"Hank, could I borrow Freddy for a while?"

"How long?"

"Less than an hour."

"Sure, if he says it's OK."

Freddy, who had heard, ambled over. "What do you want?"

"No big deal," said Hardy, "and there's five dollars in it for you."

"Hell," said Hank, "I'll do it."

"What I want you to do, Freddy, is take this envelope and walk down to Lincoln Center and hang around the fountain. I'll be about a block behind you, but when you see me don't talk to me or even act like you know me. If after fifteen minutes you don't see me or if you do see me and I don't talk to you, bring the envelope back here and give it to Hank to put away for me. Here's the envelope and here's the five."

"Gee," said the kid, "sounds just like a spy movie."

"Go. Go."

111

Hank looked like he wanted to ask some questions but luckily he got busy with customers. A minute after the boy had gone, Hardy followed.

Freddy was looking at some posters and playing the game very well. The Duchess stood in front of the fountain impatiently smoking one of her small cigars.

Hardy sauntered up to her. "Nice day."

"This is getting too foolish."

"The library is back that way. Please go there and I'll join you as soon as I can."

She said something in a language he didn't understand and turned and strode toward the library.

When she was out of sight, Hardy took the envelope from Freddy and followed her to the library. Just inside the door he gave her the envelope. "Look these over."

"Here?" she demanded.

"What better place for both of us?"

She adjusted her monocle and started reading. Patiently she examined each document. Once they had to move when the guard told them they were blocking the door. They moved to the other side of the information desk. When she was through there was a glimmer of a smile. "Excellent, except . . ."

Hardy felt a touch of panic. "Except what?"

"There seems to be a slight discrepancy in our friend's blood type. His R.O.T.C. and Army records don't agree on that one little fact."

Hardy worried. "For a minute you had me worried. That just means some medical technician didn't know what he was doing. According to my Army dog tags my blood type is O, but later on when I gave blood to the Red Cross, I found out it was B. Look." And he dug in his pockets and brought out his medical bracelet to show her. She examined the bracelet and handed it back to him.

"Sounds plausible. It's a good thing for you that you were never wounded."

He smiled weakly.

"All right," she said. "What about the rest?"

"First we check this envelope."

The monocle flashed. "That is going to extremes."

"Nothing to do with me, Duchess, library rules."

They checked the envelope and then went into a record alcove. "Do you have the money?"

She opened her purse and showed him an envelope which she slit open with one of her long violet nails. Hardy wanted to count it but he didn't. He was too nervous. All he wanted to do was to get it over with. "I'll take your word that it's all there."

"The rest."

"Walter Henry was a United States Government agent. He had certain information that was wanted by the other side . . . which I believe to be you. Whether he delivered that information or it was taken from him, or what, I don't know, and I don't want to. And now I have to admit I also don't know who killed him. It's a tossup as far as I'm concerned whether it was you or his own people. That's the whole thing."

He held his breath.

"It's enough for me." She handed him the envelope and he gave her the check tag. "It has been a pleasure knowing you and doing business with you. I hope this is not the end, and that you will not become a stranger. I have become very fond of you and, despite some of your shortcomings, I am very impressed with the way you handled the whole situation."

She brushed his lips with hers and went to pick up her envelope.

He tucked the money into his inside jacket pocket and waited until she left the library, then he scooted back into the reading room and used the elevator there to take him downstairs and out the other side of the building. He had a taxi drive him to his bank where he placed the twenty thousand (which was all there) in his safety deposit box and spent the rest of the day sitting in the Radio City Music Hall and not seeing the movie.

When it was dark he took a cab ten blocks past his house and walked back. As he walked he amused himself with the realization that all his security methods of the day were all just an exercise. Unless he were to leave town right now they could get him anytime they wanted to, if they wanted to.

There could have been dozens of eyes watching from the park or other concealed places. It didn't matter. What did matter at the moment was being inside.

And as simple as opening and closing his doors, he was.

114

He checked out the apartment. Except for Holmes and himself it was empty. He locked all the locks, set all the alarms, gorged himself on a large can of corned beef hash and went to bed.

Chapter Ten

He awoke in the middle of the night. The sleep had straightened his mind a bit. It wasn't over yet. Phase one was over. Phase two was yet to begin, and he didn't have an inkling as to how to go about implementing it.

He couldn't sleep, so he read. In the morning he still didn't have a plan for his next move.

He knew he should let Foxx know what had happened.

He dialed Manhattan North. Twenty rings later he dialed police information.

"Police Headquarters."

"Hello. Can you give me the number for Manhattan North, please?"

"Thank you," she said and then there was a pause while she seemed to be looking it up.

When she gave him the number he said, "Well, that's what I thought. I've been dialing it and it's been ringing . . ."

"Hold on, hon, I'll see if I can connect you."

"OK. Thank you."

Two rings and he was connected.

"Manhattan North, mumble, mumble, mumble."

"Detective Gerald Friday, please."

After more waiting time he heard Friday's derisive tones. "Well, if it isn't the great Private Detective Patrick Hardy calling this humble public servant. The lowly cop he threw out of his apartment with a lot of sarcastic remarks."

"Enough. Enough. Any more and I'll have to report you for police brutality."

"You get funnier every hundred years. Enough of this crap. I've got a busy day. What do you want?"

"You know those people who asked you to come and see me the last time?"

"Yeah."

"Tell them to get in touch."

"What am I—a messenger service?"

"All right. Tell me who to call at the commissioner's office and I'll take care of it myself."

"Nobody likes a smart-ass., Hardy. I'll see what I can do." And he hung up without saying goodbye.

It didn't take ten minutes for Archibald to call and tell him to go to the phone booth.

"Yes, Mr. Hardy, what can I do for you?"

"You might tell Mr. Foxx that I'm keeping my conjectures to myself but that I have some actions to report."

"We know all about them."

"I figured you might."

"Mr. Hardy, why don't you take a walk uptown and visit the Soldiers' and Sailors' Memorial, it's on . . ."

"I know where it is. Oh joy, more fun and games with you guys."

During his walk he stopped long enough at a drinking fountain to wash down a tranquilizer.

The same sort of rigamarole with different cars brought him to 35th Street and Mr. Foxx's office.

Through the cigar smoke the fat man said, "Very well, Mr. Hardy. You are here. Report."

"First," said Hardy, taking an envelope out of his jacket pocket. "It would be better for all concerned if you had these."

Foxx opened the envelope and took out the three TOP SECRET pages. He let Archibald see what they were and then placed them on his desk. "How did you acquire these?"

"I think you know."

"Let us assume that I don't. Your report please. Remember, no conjectures, actions."

"Those papers were part of a batch I found in Walter Henry's apartment. The other papers merely gave me bits of information about Walter Henry's life. Those I used to my own advantage."

"Meaning?"

"I gave them to the duchess. She was very pleased with them, and since she doesn't mind my conjecturing, I conjectured for her. She was pleased with that, too. My assignment for her is over and she says she would like us to remain friends and she would like to use my services again."

Foxx adjusted his large bulk in his chair. "What exactly did you say to her?"

Hardy told him.

"Did you tell her anything about these papers?"

"No. I figured giving them to her or even mentioning them to her might constitute an act of treason, and I'm not ready for that right now. . . . Even if that's what you meant me to do."

"What on earth are you babbling about?"

"Forgive me for conjecturing, but you asked for it. It seems very strange to me that those papers appeared just when I needed them. So either I'm a very lucky person, or somebody planted them so I could find them. Need I say more?"

"No, Mr. Hardy, I think you've said quite enough for one day. Goodbye."

Hardy got up. "If it *was* you, don't you think a strongbox hidden under the floor is a bit much?"

"Archibald, get him out of here."

As Hardy was being ushered out he said, "Somebody was very careless. Did you know that Henry's R.O.T.C. records and his Army records list different blood types?"

When he got home he still didn't know how to play his next move. He decided not to make any move

119

at all, and retreated into his private world of food, books and TV.

It was a full week later that he spotted the first commercial. The product it was pitching was a deodorant and it showed a boss yelling at a group of secretaries while the voice-over told the world that the deodorant would protect them even during the most stressful times. The interesting thing about it was that it had Linda Lee, Gerrie Hayes and Solveig Jensen as the secretaries. Hardy tried Linda's number but her service picked up. He left word that he had called.

He kept seeing a lot of the commercial until one day on a whim he hooked up his TV tape recorder and taped it. After running it over and over he realized what had caught his eye. There was a shot that really didn't blend in with the rest of the commercial. It seemed to at first glance, but it really didn't. In the shot the camera was looking over the angry boss' shoulder and over the frustrated secretaries' shoulders and onto their steno pads.

After much deliberation about going out, Hardy got dressed and took the tape to a lab where he had the section he was interested in translated to sixteen millimeter film. Then he had the one frame blown up into a still. When he was done he went to the library.

The books there weren't enough to help him out.

He called Macker. "Hi, Pat, how's it going?"

"It doesn't go, you have to push it."

"You must be all right if you have nerve enough to pull an old and crappy line like that."

"Steve, that secretary friend of yours, if I show her something and it's what I think it is, can she be trusted to keep her mouth shut?"

"That's a pretty involved sentence, Pat, but if you're asking if I trust her, yes."

"Does she do speedwriting or Gregg shorthand?"

"I don't know."

"Call her and find out for me, and if she does Gregg, ask her if I could come over and see her for a minute or two. I'm in a phone booth." And he gave him the number.

"Yes," said Hardy, barely letting the phone ring.

"She said yes to both questions. Her office is at 1515 Broadway. I'll meet you in front of the building in twenty minutes."

"Steve, you don't have to bother."

"I want to. I'm curious. Besides, as long as I was calling I told her I'd take her out to eat after work."

Donna Bradley looked exactly as Hardy expected her to look and he made a mental note to renew the acquaintance after this situation was cleared up.

She explained to him that everyone wrote Gregg differently, adding their own shortcuts and symbols, but she would give it a try.

She couldn't read it all, but what she could decipher was more than enough.

"Stop. That's it."

Macker had picked up on it too. "I shouldn't ask, but I will. Is that the same as what we found in the . . . ?"

Hardy nodded.

"You have a very hot potato, my hapless friend."

Hardy's stomach untightened for the first time in over a week. "Things are not always what they seem. Thank you, Donna. Thanks, Steve."

Back at home his service told him that Linda had called. He called back.

"Hello."

"Hi, it's me, Pat."

"Hi. My service told me you called, but I was away for the weekend."

"I thought we might get together."

"How about tonight?" she said. "Or am I being too anxious?"

"No more than I am. Let's say my place at seven."

"Uhuh. It's my turn to cook dinner. As much as I dig your gym, let's say my place at seven-thirty."

Submerging the fractional doubts he had about her, he said her place would be fine. When he hung up he put the tape and film in his safe. Phase two had taken care of itself. Phase three was about to begin.

She didn't live too far from him. Central Park West, near the Dakota.

They kissed like longtime lovers and she sat him down and gave him a scotch on the rocks.

He drank. "How've you been?"

"Pretty good. You?"

There was a long silence while they sat there.

Hardy lit a cigarette. Finished his drink. Put out his cigarette. "Where's the bedroom?"

She answered him by taking his hand and leading

him to the room where the covers of the bed were already turned down and waiting for them.

Following their frenetic lovemaking they took a shower together and she gave him another drink.

From the armchair he was sitting in he could see her. She had given him a red and yellow Oriental robe to wear. She was wearing only enough to keep splattering food from burning her. "That's quite a costume you've got on," he said, referring to the long apron that covered her front, but left her rear in view.

"You should see some I've worn," she giggled. "You know the old gag about whether or not the Chinese girl's is vertical like everyone else's, or horizontal? Well, when I first started I worked for a sharpshooter around Gary and places like that. He'd shoot targets out of my hands and clay pipes out of my mouth or dishes I would roll across the stage. . . . But the finish was when I came out at the end wearing as little as Indiana law would allow and I had a plate with a vertical line on it over my crotch. He would shoot and miss. And he'd shoot and miss again. Then I would raise my hand for him to stop and I would turn the plate so the line was horizontal. Bang. He fired. It broke. Big laugh. Big finish."

Hardy chuckled and walked into the kitchen. "Didn't it hurt?" he said, rubbing her belly and below.

"You keep doing that and you won't get any dinner. No, on that shot he fired blanks. I had a hidden mechanism that broke the plate. Get out of here."

123

"I saw that commercial you and the other girls did. Very good. You do that for Raven, Thompson and Peck?"

"Uh huh. Mrs. de Montespan got it for me. Soup's on. Ready or not, here comes mama."

The soup was bean curd soup, followed by roast pork with Chinese celery cabbage and diced chicken with vegetables. She complimented him on his use of chopsticks. "Not many high noses really know how to eat with them, they just think they do."

"High noses?"

"Caucasians."

Hardy ate and ate and ate.

Linda watched him and smiled. "My mother would really be impressed with you. She told me that back in China when many suitors came courting the one who ate the most bowls of rice was usually thought as the most worthy. You've had three bowls so far."

When they had their tea, she winced when he asked for sugar.

"Sorry. I like sugar in my tea. Hope I haven't disappointed you."

"Just where tea drinking is concerned," and she kissed him on the neck.

After dinner they watched television and she served him rice cakes and sesame candy.

This time their lovemaking was less frantic and more tender. Hardy had no urgent needs to explode, but rather a wish to keep on going forever just on the brink of climax.

Climax they did, and again. Then they cuddled. On

the radio Helen Reddy gave way to a lush rendition of "You Go To My Head" followed by Peggy Lee telling him to find somebody to love, because "You're Nobody Till Somebody Loves You." And he slept.

In the morning they made love again and she was off to a modeling job. Automatically he started to snoop around. After rummaging through the first closet he grew annoyed with himself and quit. Without even stopping for breakfast he left the apartment, slamming the door behind him.

Later when they talked on the phone she told him she had to go to Baltimore for several days for a job. "But there's a big party on Fire Island on Friday. Would you like to take me?"

"Sure thing. Who's throwing it?"

"I don't know. A woman I know, Sally Hunter, told me about it."

"Is it all right for me to come?"

"Sure. She told me to bring a date, then if I got tired of him I could trade him in."

"Oh, is that the kind of parties you get invited to?"

"Who said I was invited? Nobody is ever invited to these things. You just hear about them and go. It's this guy's big party of the year. He even has a bunch of seaplanes leaving from the East River to take you there. No guest list or anything. If you know about it, and you know where the planes leave from, you just get on and go. Sometimes the weirdest people just stumble onto it and go."

"I'll bet."

125

"See you Friday. I'll come to your place straight from Baltimore. . . . Don't worry I'll call first, so you can get rid of whatever woman you have there with you."

"You act like you think I'm a sex fiend."

"What do you mean think? I know."

"Just to keep you guessing I'll pick you up at your place."

"OK, stinker," she said, "around noon. Ciao."

He called Laura and arranged for her to keep Holmes with her from Thursday on.

All the while Mrs. Sally Hunter kept nagging at him. What did she have to do with all of this? He suspected this weekend had something to do with all of this.

Of course he could be getting more paranoic and the weekend could merely be what Linda told him it was and Sally Hunter knowing Gerrie and Linda was just one big New York coincidence. Sure it was.

He called Steve Macker. Steve's service told him that he would be out of town until next week.

A quick thought popped into Hardy's mind about calling Donna Bradley, but he unpopped it and tried to concentrate on the matter at hand. He called Alice, but at the store they said she had taken the next two weeks off. She wasn't home either.

"Macker, you slimey . . ." He thought about calling Donna again. No.

He lay down on the chaise to concentrate and he sat up almost immediately. But he could call Gerrie Hayes.

According to her service, she too was out of town until next week. Maybe he had misjudged Macker?

Maybe Alice was just off somewhere on her own? Maybe Macker was working? Maybe Gerrie Hayes was . . . ? Maybe Linda was . . . ? Maybe Sally Hunter was . . . ? Maybe Fire Island was . . . ? Maybe? Maybe? Maybe?

What a stupid idiot he was. A lot of what he had in mind was all conjecture, but there was one thing he could verify. He searched out Walter Henry's photo and caught the first train he could to Bayshore. From there to the ferry. As luck would have it the cop he had spoken to the last time was at the dock. Hardy showed him the picture, the man nodded that he thought it looked like the man that had washed ashore. Hardy thanked him and rushed to catch the same ferry back. Halfway across he realized he should have asked him whether he knew anything about the big party coming up that weekend. Well, it wasn't that important. He would find out soon enough.

He tried to reach Alice that night and again on Wednesday morning. He worked out halfheartedly and after breakfast spent his time watching TV and browsing through *The Complete Sherlock Holmes.*

It was raining. He tried Alice again. He was ready to forget phase three and whatever phase came after that and tell Alice what Foxx wanted him to, that he was unable to figure out who had killed her uncle. Then he would leave word for Linda that he couldn't make it, and then take the thirty thousand and go to Paris or somewhere and forget about Walter Henry and the duchess and Korboff and Claude and Foxx and Archibald and Linda and Fire Island and the whole stupid thing.

There was no answer.

He could leave anyway.

Or he could wait for Friday and let whatever was going to happen happen.

He took a tranquilizer.

He could call Sally Hunter.

Or . . . Solveig Jensen.

He dialed information for her number. "It's in mid-town somewhere."

"I have a Solveig Jensen on East 16th Street."

"That's it, Operator."

When she had given him the number he said, "What was that complete address again, Operator?"

"I'm sorry, but we are not allowed to give out that information."

He hung up and went through the entire process again.

"What is that full address, Operator?"

This one was more cooperative.

Then, for what seemed no reason at all, instead of calling he decided to go downtown and see her.

As he locked his front door behind him, Hardy knew that part of his mind had been planning this all along while he was trying to find out her address, but he wasn't sure if it was prompted by his mind or his nerves or his gonads.

With that last thought in mind he regretted taking the tranquilizer.

The cabdriver got caught in the maze created by the park and Beth Israel Hospital and was unable to make a left turn.

"I'll have to go to 14th Street and come around."

"Forget it, driver. I'll get out here and walk."

It was a nice little park and it had stopped raining so he was tempted to sit down and sit awhile. Ignoring the damp bench, he did.

Ten minutes later he was fidgeting, and he got up and continued on his way.

He rang the downstairs bell and in a few seconds got an answering buzz.

She opened the door to the width of the chain bolt. "Oh, I know you," and she opened the door to let him in.

She was completely nude.

"Come inside, I'm getting some sun." He followed her into a room and instinctively put an arm in front of his eyes. "I'm sorry, here are some glasses."

He adjusted the goggles while she kept talking. "I love having a tan body. Any chance I have I'm at the beach. When I don't have a chance or it rains or it's cloudy, I use the lamps. Would you care to join me? I remember where I know you from. You're a friend of Madame de Montespan. Are you in the business?"

"I beg your pardon?"

"Are you in the same business Madame de Montespan is in?"

"You might say that."

"Come on, undress and get some sun. It's good for you."

129

"What the hell," thought Hardy, and he took off his clothes, laying them neatly on the chair. She seemed to be only interested in cooking her body and paid no attention to him at all.

Except when he was through. "You have a good physique. I like that in a man. There's a mat over there in the corner. Bring it over and lie down next to me and we can talk."

And they talked. About absolutely nothing. They chatted utter nonsense for about ten minutes and then stopped only long enough to turn over. Less than ten minutes later she stood up and turned out the lamps.

"You're very white, and too much the first time is no good. Do you want to look at my pictures?"

Hardy pulled the goggles down around his neck and stared blankly. "Yeah, sure. Why not? You have anything to drink?"

"In the kitchen."

He found the kitchen and poured himself a glass of orange juice and rejoined her in the middle of the floor where she had a half dozen or so large photo books out. She sipped some of his drink and they sat there and looked at her in hundreds of different nude poses.

It was silly. The silliest part of it was that, though he dug her body, her complete nonchalance had put a kind of damper on him. But those pictures. Solveig sitting. Solveig standing. Solveig bathing. Solveig cupping her breasts. Solveig with her butt up in the air. Solveig lying on a leopard rug.

She finished his orange juice and then just as casually she lay on her back on the floor and said, "Do you want to make it now?"

And they did. Goggles and all.

She was good. But it was like a tennis game. Very well played and very skilled and agile with a lot of fancy serves and returns.

When it was over she stretched and yawned and said, "Thank you. That was very nice, but I think you'd better go now."

She was back under the lamps. He slipped his goggles on while he dressed, and was just tucking in his shirt when he heard the key in the lock.

Before he could move Claude walked in.

"You bastard. You dare to play around with my woman!" And she was charging. Hardy turned one of the lamps toward Claude. While she was momentarily blinded, he grabbed his jacket and ran past her and out the door and down the stairs. He didn't dare wait for the elevator and he didn't stop moving or looking over his shoulder until he was well past 25th Street. Only then did he realize people were staring at him. He smiled stupidly and snatched the goggles from his face and stuffed them into his pocket.

He found a candy store and had an egg cream along with another tranquilizer.

He was hungry.

Corned beef and french fries and a cream soda in a delicatessen took care of this and then he started walking again.

Chapter Eleven

When he got home he fed Holmes an early supper and went out again. He got his VW from the garage and just started driving. He needed to think.

This last near thing with Claude was it. These people were too much for him. He would quit. He'd return Alice's money and send her a telegram telling her he was quitting the case. Another telegram to Linda telling her he was sorry but other things had come up.

He pulled over to the side of the road and dry swallowed a tranquilizer.

Laura was taking care of Holmes so he didn't have to worry about that.

Where the hell was he?

Connecticut.

Why not? He would drive up to Maine and find a lonely area and spend a week or so by himself. Then with everything thought out he would come back.

Then he'd take Holmes and pack a few bags and . . .

He was very tired.

He stopped at the first motel he saw.

Connecticut TV gave him the bonus of *The Thief of Bagdad* and at the end he agreed with Sabu and wished he too could have a magic carpet to go flying off on in search of fun.

A large breakfast of bacon and eggs and pancakes and two cups of coffee did wonders for his stomach and his soul. He picked up a New York newspaper without really looking at it and folded it under his arm. He went back to his room to read the paper and perhaps fall asleep.

On the front page was a face he knew. A very pretty face. And he remembered how blond she was and how agile.

The headline read: NUDE MODEL FOUND STRANGLED

Solveig Jensen was dead.

Claude had killed Solveig Jensen.

The paper didn't say so, but he knew. The paper used a lot of words to say very little. But it did mention a man being seen running from the apartment. The man was described as wearing a mask. Hardy imagined they meant him and the sun goggles he had worn.

133

Tiredly he reached for the phone and dialed Manhattan North in New York.

"Friday speaking."

"Hello, this is Pat Hardy."

"What do you want, Private Detective?"

"I was just reading about a murder that happened yesterday. The model . . ."

"I am not working on that case. How many times do I have to . . ."

"Friday, I know who killed the girl."

"OK, Private Detective. Who?"

"A dyke by the name of Claude. She was the blond's lover."

"And how do you know all this, Private Detective?"

"Because I was there."

"Is that a fact? . . . Well, I tell you what. Why don't you come and see me and we'll . . ."

Hardy stopped listening. What a fool he had been! Friday never talked that slowly in his whole life. They must be tracing the call. He was still talking.

". . . I'll be in my office all day. What time do you want to make it for?"

Hardy's mind was in slow motion. "Uh, two ought to be fine. Yeah, two o'clock."

"OK. Two o'clock it is. Oh, I meant to ask you."

Hardy finally snapped out of it. "I'll talk to you about it when I see you. Goodbye." And he disconnected.

He didn't know much about call tracing, but he

figured that if they had tried they would know at least the call had come from Connecticut.

He checked out and drove back toward New York on the Turnpike. They'd never figure him to come back. But they might. What a stupid fool he was! They didn't even have him connected with it, but his big stupid mouth had taken care of that. Now he had to see this thing through whether he wanted to or not.

Of course he could be panicking for nothing. Maybe he should just go in and give his statement and that would be it. Of course it would.

They'd book him for murder. And the way things looked he could be convicted.

Even if they believed him about Claude, they might hold him as a material witness. No. He had to be outside. He had to straighten out this whole stupid mess himself.

The answer had to be on Fire Island. It had to be. It better be, because he couldn't think of anything else. Now he had to go to Fire Island.

If they had figured out that he was in Connecticut they might be checking all roads in. He took an exit off and then drove back till he picked up the route to Boston.

In Boston he parked the car in a garage and bought a mustache and a beard in a men's salon. Then he went to a drugstore and bought a pair of scissors, a mirror, and sunglasses.

At the train station he sat in a dirty toilet stall and cut the beard up and flushed it away. Then he

135

reshaped the large mustache and put it on. The mustache and the glasses and a part in his hair where he never had one seemed to do the trick.

He bought a ticket for the next train which was due any minute. After he got on and the train was just about to pull out, he got off. The trouble with Patrick Hardy was that, despite everything, he loved playing detective.

Between the cab and the shuttle plane he was in New York in less than an hour. Too late for his appointment with Detective Friday. That was too bad. What was worse, he didn't know what to do next. If he called his apartment someone might be listening in.

There was nothing in the *Post* about him, and very little more on Solveig Jensen's murder. Some other catastrophe had taken its place and it was now relegated to two columns on the inside that simply rehashed the old information.

Fire Island. Once out there he could wrap it all up . . . he hoped.

What was Friday doing?

And where the hell was he going to spend the night?

Ruby was out of town.

Linda was out of town.

Donna Bradley.

He would take Donna Bradley out, and then he would take Donna Bradley home. And then . . .

But he couldn't go wearing the silly mustache.

Hardy checked his bag in a locker and went to

1515 Broadway. He waited for an empty elevator. While it took him up to Donna Bradley's office he peeled the mustache and shoved it into his pocket. Another rider entered just as he was rubbing his upper lip with his handkerchief.

The receptionist told Donna someone was there to see her. "Hi. Oh, I remember you, you're Steve's friend."

"Yeah, well I was just passing by and I thought I might drop in and see if you were doing anything for dinner."

"As a matter of fact, I did have a date to go shopping with my girlfriend."

"Oh."

"But I can break it. Excuse me, I have to run, that's my boss buzzing for me. Meet you downstairs by the escalator . . . five-thirty."

He went downstairs rubbing his hands and smiling.

The rest of the afternoon he spent reading in the 42nd Street library.

He took her to the same place he had taken Alice. Many daiquiries and a fine French dinner later, Hardy was glowing with alcohol and confidence. In the cab he thought about what she might be like in bed. She thanked him for a marvelous dinner and said good night to him at the door.

Now what?

That night a "Mr. Mike Easy" slept in a crummy midtown hotel alone, with a chair propped under the doorknob.

Friday.

With his mustache back on he picked up his bag at the locker, bought a paper and went to Linda Lee's apartment.

When she told him to come up, he hopped on the elevator and removed the mustache again. He rang her bell.

"Hi," she said, embracing him, "where've you been?"

"What do you mean?"

"Well, I got back a day sooner than I expected and tried to reach you yesterday but your service didn't know where you were."

Hardy stared at her in disbelief. "You came back one day early."

"That's right. Pat, what's wrong? You don't look too well."

"I'll tell you about it sometime. Did you hear about Solveig?"

"Yes. It's horrible. This city scares me more and more. They don't seem to know who did it."

"Honey, if you don't mind, I'm going to take a shower and then we have some serious talking to do."

"OK, Pat, does that mean you're going to propose?"

"I'm afraid not."

"Good. I was afraid you were going to spoil a beautiful relationship." And she sat down to read the paper he had brought with him.

While he was showering and shaving he decided that it would be silly to tell Linda anything she didn't need to know. And if she were more involved than he thought, it might be damned stupid and he had done enough stupid things so far.

He wrapped himself in a towel and came out. "Anything new in the paper about Solveig?"

"No. What was that serious talking bit all about?"

"Nothing that can't wait. I guess I should get dressed so we can catch our plane."

"It's nothing that can't wait," she said, tugging at his towel. "We can always catch the next one."

Chapter Twelve

When they got downstairs a cab was just letting someone out. They piled in, bags and all, and Linda told the driver to take them to the dock at the East River and 23rd Street.

The slat plane trip didn't take long. They shared the ride with two young men dressed in identical outfits of purple suede who didn't talk to each other, nor to them. This was fine with Hardy. He and Linda held hands and looked at the view.

As the pilot was preparing to land, Hardy searched in his pockets for his tranquilizers. All that was left in the pill bottle was a lonely piece of cotton.

When the plane did land a bunch of servant types with wagons were there at the dock. Linda said to one, "Put those bags in my room. . . . Come on, Pat, I'll give you the tour."

That remark about the luggage didn't ring too well to Pat. Linda certainly didn't sound like just another uninvited guest.

As they passed the tennis courts they saw Gerrie Hayes playing with Ludwig Lerche. Curious and curiouser, thought Hardy.

There was a general bit of waving at one another and Linda said, "You know Gerrie, and the man she's playing with is your host, Ludwig Lerche. Isn't that a funny name for a Negro?"

Hardy didn't answer. And curiouser, he thought.

"And this is the Sunken Forest," she said as they walked on wooden walks that threaded through a series of weird-looking trees.

"This is the only National Park that's below sea level."

Hardy nodded. "Does it ever get flooded?"

"I don't know," said Linda, "I guess it could during a bad storm. Those sand dunes form sort of a sea wall."

"Like the dikes in Holland," he said.

"Oh, you'll find plenty of those around here too."

They both laughed at her silly joke and kept walking.

Hardy's stomach growled. "I'm starved. When and where do we eat?"

"There are places in town, or we could go to the house."

"Let's go to the house, by all means."

141

When Hardy and Linda walked into the dining room, there they were. The duchess, Korboff and Claude. Gerrie Hayes. And Ludwig Lerche and Sally Hunter.

As he rethought the phrase curious and curiouser, he thought of Alice Henry and at this moment wished he had never met her.

Ludwig Lerche spoke. "Hello, Linda. So nice to see you again, Mr. Hardy. Please sit down. We're all just about to have a late lunch."

Hardy nodded at Mr. Lerche and sat, but all his awareness was concentrated on the duchess and Claude.

"Hello, darling," said the duchess, "I'm sure this is going to be a wonderful weekend." She placed a small cigar in her mouth which Korboff lit.

Claude glared and Hardy tried not to look at her.

The baked red snapper served with grapefruit was very good, but Hardy ate automatically and didn't ask for seconds.

When lunch was over the people that most concerned Hardy sort of disappeared, but by that time all sorts of new people started drifting in. And soon the air was redolent with booze and pot and other such sundry things.

"Isn't this crazy?" said Linda.

"A bit much for me," he said. "Couldn't we get out of it for a while?"

"We could go to our room."

"Fine."

But somebody had already appropriated their

142

room, and their bed. Back out into the madding crowd they went.

Sally Hunter was standing on a table. "Look at me, everybody. Look at me."

Some did and some didn't, but that didn't bother icy Sally Hunter, who wasn't icy any more. She took off her blouse and while she caressed her own brassiered breasts she marched around the table. "Not enough? Well, there's more." And she removed one breast from its confinement and started squeezing it, very hard. "You want to do that? Who wants to do that?"

A man started to mount the table, but she pushed him off.

"Not yet. This little beauty's got a sister. Do you want to see it? Say yes."

By this time she had the attention she wanted.

"Yes," said the crowd, and she tore off her bra.

Then she started her own little dance. It wasn't graceful, but the meaning was clear. And as she danced she caressed herself, and pinched herself.

Then she stopped. "Here it comes."

She removed her long skirt.

The crowd moaned its disapproval; she was wearing panties.

"Be patient, sweethearts." And she rubbed herself between her legs. She started to moan softly. "Soon. Soon."

Then, almost maniacally, she pulled off her panties.

Then she got down on all fours and yelled, "Come and get it."

And the table was besieged. Those who couldn't get at the many opportunities Sally offered went at each other.

Hardy was excited, but disgusted. His idea of an orgy was lots of women and him. "Let's go."

Linda smiled weakly and nodded.

Outside they walked along the beach silently.

"Pat?"

"What?"

"Mr. Lerche has another house that nobody knows about. It's probably empty. We could go there."

"That sounds like a good idea."

"It sounds like a very good idea," said the duchess, who was suddenly twisting Linda's arm behind her with one hand and holding a knife at her throat with the other.

"Joseph," she whispered behind her, "tell Lerche. My darling Pat Hardy will give me no trouble whatsoever. Will you, darling?"

"No. Lead on, Duchess."

"After you, my pet, I'll tell you the way."

The duchess sat Linda in one chair and had Hardy sit in another.

While they waited the duchess kept threatening Linda's face with the knife.

"Cut that out, Duchess."

"If you had considered the humor of that remark you might never have said it. Then again, darling, you always did have a good sense of humor."

"Not now I don't. . . . Stop that."

"I won't hurt your precious plaything. Would I do that to you, Linda darling?"

Linda swallowed as best she could.

"Would I, darling?"

"No."

"Goddamn it," Hardy exploded. "Stop torturing the girl."

Korboff came running in, with Claude trailing behind him.

"Well, Joseph?" asked the duchess.

"Mr. Lerche says he'll be here as soon as he can and not to do a thing until he arrives."

"Nonsense. I'll do as I please." Then to Hardy, "Darling, you and I could have had a wonderful relationship together, but . . . Joseph . . . get rid of him."

"No," said Claude, "he's mine."

"Very well then, both of you. Kill him together, then weigh him down and toss him in the water. I'll take care of the girl. After all, why shouldn't I have my pleasure too?"

Hardy's fears and reflexes were fighting each other. If he had been alone he would have been at them all by now, but Linda was a factor those Army psychologists hadn't considered.

His system never had a chance to decide. Korboff hit him behind the ear and he was out.

He was still alive. He opened his eyes and saw Korboff and Claude sharing a cigarette. As they passed it back and forth he could smell the marijuana.

"Good. You're awake," said Claude. "Now the fun begins."

Hardy was oriented now: they were in the Sunken Forest.

"Korboff and I are going to have a little contest. Which one of us gets to kill you. You are in the middle. Get up. There is no sport if you are not ready. You are in the middle. I am here." And she moved into position. "And Korboff is there." And he moved. "Now it is your choice, Mr. Hardy. Which one of us shall kill you." She dropped the marijuana cigarette and tensed, ready for action.

Korboff, more relaxed, was waiting too.

When Hardy didn't move at all, Claude grew impatient and moved in on him.

Hardy's mind was confused again. He knew she was tougher than most men . . . but she was a woman. A part of his mind also noted that Korboff was staying out of this and smoking another cigarette. Forget Korboff. More important was Claude who was rushing toward him like a bull at a matador. He avoided her first onslaught, but not completely. The ringing in his left ear told him she had clipped him. A quick look at Korboff. Still watching and waiting.

This time when Claude charged again, the male-female morality was gone. Hardy was all reflexes. But he had been paying too much attention to Korboff. She landed on him full force knocking him to the ground, her hands around his throat. Even as he moved to save his life he couldn't help comparing the battle to some perverse form of sex.

One hand was free, but where to use it . . . ? His

hand found a hard breast, and then a nipple. Gasping for air he pinched and twisted.

Claude yelled in pain and relaxed her hold long enough for Hardy to roll out from under.

In a second he was behind her and in several more seconds he had snapped her neck.

Korboff!

Hardy dropped Claude's limp body and started racing toward Korboff who was racing toward him. At the right moment Hardy propelled his body at him feet first and knocked the man to the ground.

Korboff was stunned, but Hardy's bad knee had suffered too.

Those reflexes never seemed to consider that weak cartilage. He knew that in a short time the leg would be swollen with fluid.

Korboff was up and coming toward him.

He was almost on him.

Hardy braced himself on his hands and shot his good right leg into Korboff's crotch. The man screamed in pain and his own momentum sent him catapulting over Hardy's body.

Hardy turned, breathing hard, ready for Korboff's next move. There was none. Cautiously he limped over. Just at the point Korboff's head hit the ground was a very lovely-looking rock. Korboff's head was smashed like an egg.

Hardy's leg was swollen and he knew that the fluid in his knee had blood in it. He knew that if he made it, eventually some sadistic doctor would have to stick a needle in that knee and aspirate it.

Figuring he could swim better than he could walk, he crawled for the dunes and the water. He shook as he crawled and realized that the wetness in his pants was not sweat, but urine. He was thankful his bowels had stayed tight.

Somehow he managed to make his way back to the house.

Only to have Ludwig Lerche kick him in the bad knee.

Chapter Thirteen

A blue blur and a black blur. When his eyes came into focus he saw the duchess and Lerche looking at him.

Hardy saw Linda sitting in the same chair, in a daze.

He sneezed.

"I think the poor boy has a cold," said the duchess.

"Yes," said Lerche, "but a shot of penicillin should knock that cold right out of him. How fortunate for you that I happen to have some with me."

It was then Hardy realized he was tied down to a long narrow table.

"No. That's a stupid way to do it," said the duchess, brandishing her knife.

Lerche slapped her. "Be quiet. You've made enough blunders as it is."

The duchess' monocle flew to the floor and Lerche turned his attention back to Hardy. "Where are Claude and Korboff?"

"Dead."

"Are you bragging . . . ? No, I think not. A pity to lose them, but since I didn't want you to die that way, it's all just as well. You see, when Annette reported to me . . . She does report to me, you know. When she reported to me about your allergy to penicillin, I thought what a marvelous way to kill a man. According to my research, if you are truly allergic you should first go into anaphylactic shock. Your face will get blotchy and then your complexion will become sallow. There will be shallow breathing, your blood pressure will go way down . . ."

A quirky thought of how happy that would make Merle Doyle passed through Hardy's brain.

Lerche kept droning on and on, "Your pulse will beat rapidly but very faintly, and you should go into irreversible shock in three hours. In four you should be dead. Of course if a doctor got to you before three hours he could save you with some adrenaline and Pennicillinace and antihistamines, but I doubt that that will happen."

He kept the needle in the air and squirted a drop of fluid to clear the hypodermic of air. "Wouldn't do to kill you with an air bubble, that is not the object of the experiment."

Neither Hardy nor Lerche saw the duchess, but Linda did.

"I want to kill him my way," screamed the duchess and attacked Hardy with the knife. Linda leaped at the duchess and grabbed her hand, but the duchess was too strong for her. She stabbed Linda in the heart.

In a rage Lerche grabbed the knife from the dead girl's chest and plunged it into the duchess' throat. "Stupid bitch. You never could take orders. My way! MY way!"

Then he pushed the duchess' body away from him and sighed and smiled. "It's almost ludicrous to kill you in such a sophisticated way with all this carnage about, but one must finish what one begins."

Hardy's mind was a morass of confusion. Linda dead. The duchess dead. Both in less than seconds, and all he could think of was their warm moving bodies under him in the act of sex.

Lerche leaned over and stuck him with the needle sending the penicillin through his veins. The black man smiled down at him. "Bon Voyage, Mr. Hardy."

In one last burst of horror and fear and terror and anger Hardy tore one hand free and grabbed Lerche by the throat, and squeezed and squeezed and squeezed.

151

Chapter Fourteen

Waking up to new faces was getting to be monotonous. He spoke two words, "Penicillin. Allergic." And passed out again.

This time when he woke up he stayed awake. The doctor assured him that everything had been caught in time and left Hardy with Foxx and Archibald and Friday and Alice.

Alice spoke first. "Oh, Pat. I'm so sorry. Look at you, and it's all my fault."

"Where've you been?"

"I got uptight and took off for Mexico. But then I figured that was no good so I came back to New York to find you. When I couldn't, I got in touch with the police and they sent me to see Mr. Friday and here I am."

"And here you are, Mr. Hardy," said Mr. Foxx. "A lot of dead bodies, but as I feared, you bungled a mission my people and I have been working on for a long time. A very important mission."

"Don't worry," said Hardy, "It got out. What happened to Lerche?"

"He's dead. You killed him. The Chinese girl and the duchess too, both dead. What do you mean it got out?" All this from Archibald.

Hardy gulped in air. It felt good. But his leg hurt. "You sure you want Friday and Alice to hear?"

"Friday has clearance," said Foxx. "And if you really do know, Miss Henry has a right to know too."

"You made one major mistake, Mr. Foxx, with Walter Henry. When I looked into his life and his activities, it didn't strike me right away, but then it occurred to me that nobody could be that bland. Could I have some water?"

Alice got him some.

Hardy drank, dribbling some on his chin. "You see, Alice, nobody killed your uncle Walter Henry because you never did have an uncle Walter Henry. Don't interrupt. You had one all right, but just as you thought, he died when he was a kid. You ever see a movie called *The Man Who Never Was?* Well I did, and I'll bet Mr. Foxx saw it, or at least read the book. In it the English didn't want the Germans to know about the invasion of Sicily. So they dropped a corpse with phony papers into the water for the Germans to find. Those papers said the invasion was coming at a different place. I don't feel so good."

153

After resting a while, Hardy picked up his story. "Good old Macker. He found the important flaw. Lucky for you he was working for me and not for them. He couldn't find out anything in Travis Corners. And in Dallas he found some other papers including Walter Henry's birth certificate."

He looked at Foxx. "You must have destroyed the death certificate. Except Macker is thorough and a hunch player; he visited the grade school the Henry boys had attended. After asking some of the older teachers if they remembered who had been teaching back in the twenties he found one who did, and as a matter of fact an old teacher was a friend of hers. . . . a Mrs. MacGuffen. The younger teacher visited her old friend at an old age home as often as possible.

"Could I have some more water?

"At the home, Mrs. MacGuffen told Macker that Walter Henry had died, she forgot how, when he was twelve. Macker also found out that no one else had asked her about Walter Henry. He cautioned her and her friend not to repeat the story. They thought he was lying to them when he said it had to do with national security.

"Also, he made sure to cover his tracks so no one else could pick up on his lead. Fortunately, the duchess' people only knew about Travis Corners and not Dallas. By that time I was in the picture. . . . I'm sorry, could you get them to give me a pain killer for my knee. . . . I have to . . ."

Next time he awoke they were in a hospital.

Alice smiled at him. "How do you feel?"

"Better."

"We're in New York. They flew us in in those seaplanes."

Foxx moved his large bulk closer. "If you don't mind, Mr. Hardy, I would appreciate . . ."

"I know. The rest of the story about the fake Walter Henry."

"Not that, you blatherer. I know that. You said they got it out. How?" And he gnawed on an unlit cigar.

Hardy grinned. "I'm saving that part for last. After all, Alice is my client, not you. Using your uncle as a beginning, Mr. Foxx and his friends created a man for all purposes. Anytime they needed a cover identity for an agent he was Mr. Walter Henry. They probably have a lot more fake identities floating around, just in case. By the way, what happened to Mrs. Hunter?"

"She's in custody," said Archibald irritably. "Go on."

"You might check out Gerrie Hayes. I think she's OK, but check her out. How about you, Friend Friday, no comments?"

"I'm just listening," said the cop.

"OK," said Hardy, "they created the man Walter Henry. Even rented him an apartment and an office. And they had an agent posing as Walter Henry use the apartment and office often enough to look real. Didn't have to be the same agent. Who looks at faces in New York? Even established the dietetic jelly busi-

155

ness. I don't know if it's for real or a cover for Mr. Foxx, but that's none of my business.

"Now comes the scheme. Mr. Foxx thought of using Walter Henry as a means of passing false information to the other side which would sidetrack them in something which can't be revealed because of security. Guess I'm learning, huh, Mr. Archibald?"

No answer.

Hardy continued. "He probably thought of using a real agent, but then if he considered it, which I'm sure he did, he concluded that a real agent might be captured and might crack. So, they waited for a corpse who had died the right kind of death and had Walter Henry's established physical appearance and then quick froze it or something like that. They do wonderful things with science these days.

"Then, a live Walter Henry arranged for a meeting off the shore of Fire Island. That stuff about military installation and military posts was all garbage to explain why the police weren't looking into it. They probably cooperated with Foxx on that. Right, Friday?"

Silence.

"Walter Henry was supposed to come by small boat.

"The enemy was supposed to come by small boat.

"They were supposed to skin-dive in wet suits and exchange the carefully waterproofed documents for carefully waterproofed bills.

"At the proper time a third boat appeared, and fired shots at Walter Henry's boat.

"You know, a lot of this is conjecture on my part, so what I don't know for a fact . . ."

"You're doing admirably," said Foxx drily.

"Thank you. Praise indeed. Hey, I think I'm getting hungry."

Foxx nodded to Archibald who stepped outside the room.

"Anyway, I figure the Henry corpse was defrosted and pumped full of whole blood. At the right time an agent who was on board with the corpse shot some holes into it and tossed it overboard. Ghoulish, huh? Then the agent took off in the Walter Henry boat with the third boat in hot pursuit. As was hoped, the enemy boat took a chance and stayed to fish Walter Henry out of the water, long enough to get the fake papers from the body, then they tossed him back in.

"The duchess hired me to make sure that Walter Henry was kosher before she sent the information on to her superiors. By the way, she wasn't the boss. Lerche was."

Archibald was back in the room.

"So we gathered from Mrs. Hunter," said Foxx, "but you said they got the information out. How?"

"One more thing. Someone really wanted to make Walter Henry look authentic. So they said, let's give him a real live heir, or heiress as the case was with you, Alice. Was that your idea, Archibald? That's what brought me into it and made your life so miserable, Mr. Foxx. First you tried to stop me, then you realized you had to leave me alone. Finally, when I

157

wasn't moving fast enough, you even helped me with that strongbox in the floor of Walter Henry's apartment.

"Now the biggie. They sent the info out via a commercial made by the advertising firm of Raven, Thompson and Peck. It's been on the air for a while, might even still be running. Whether the ad agency was just used or they're part of the organization I don't know. That's for you to find out. The information was written in shorthand on the steno books of the three models in the commercial."

George Archibald glared at him. "All right, if that's it, I have to admit it, you did it. But that mess we cleaned up on the island. There must have been a better way."

"Don't chide Mr. Hardy, George," said Julius Foxx. "He preferred doing it 'the Hardy way.'" There was a hint of a grin on the fat man's face, but if it was there at all it was gone now. "Satisfactory, Mr. Hardy. Satisfactory."

"Thank you, Mr. Foxx. Oh, good. Here's my dinner. I'm starving to death."

Watch for

Red is for Murder
A Patrick Hardy Mystery
Martin Meyers

Visit

**FIND OUT WHY
THE CRITICS LOVE THE
HISTORICAL MYSTERIES OF
MAAN MEYERS**

Visit us at www.speakingvolumes.us

Award-Winning Author

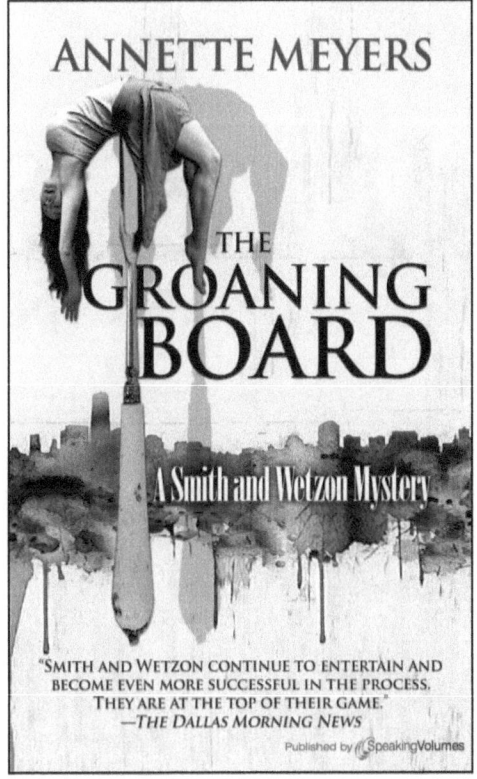

ANNETTE MEYERS

THE
GROANING
BOARD

A Smith and Wetzon Mystery

"SMITH AND WETZON CONTINUE TO ENTERTAIN AND
BECOME EVEN MORE SUCCESSFUL IN THE PROCESS.
THEY ARE AT THE TOP OF THEIR GAME."
—*THE DALLAS MORNING NEWS*

Published by SpeakingVolumes

Visit us at www.speakingvolumes.us

Award-Winning Author

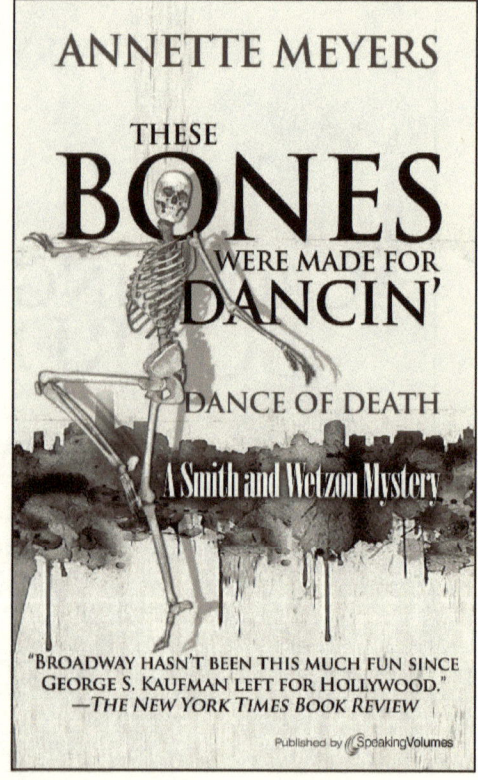

ANNETTE MEYERS

THESE
BONES
WERE MADE FOR
DANCIN'

DANCE OF DEATH

A Smith and Wetzon Mystery

"BROADWAY HASN'T BEEN THIS MUCH FUN SINCE
GEORGE S. KAUFMAN LEFT FOR HOLLYWOOD."
—*THE NEW YORK TIMES BOOK REVIEW*

Published by SpeakingVolumes

Visit us at <u>www.speakingvolumes.us</u>

Award-Winning Author
Annette Meyers

An Olivia Brown Mystery

ANNETTE
MEYERS
FREE
LOVE

Published by SpeakingVolumes

Visit us at www.speakingvolumes.us